GUNMAN, GUNMAN

Also available in Large Print
by Nelson Nye:

Red Sombrero
Riders By Night

Nelson Nye

GUNMAN, GUNMAN

G.K.HALL&CO.
Boston, Massachusetts
1990

Published in Large Print by arrangement with
Nelson Nye.

G.K. Hall Large Print Book Series.

Set in 16 pt. Plantin.

Library of Congress Cataloging in Publication Data

Nye, Nelson C. (Nelson Coral), 1907-.
    Gunman, gunman / Nelson Nye.
       p.   cm.—(G.K. Hall large print book series) (Nightingale
series)
    ISBN 0-8161-4955-0 (lg. print)
    1. Large type books. I. Title.
[PS3527.Y33G84   1990]
813'.54—dc20   89-26837

GUNMAN, GUNMAN

ONE

HER MOTHER WAS with another man in a locked back room of the Aces Up when vigilantes hanged her father for trying to make off with Jade Fiersen's horses.

When Endite saw her at the Hairpin House, she was on her own—'biscuit shooting' the cowboys called it. In the big noisy room she looked self-conscious and awkward, and was easily embarrassed. He could see right away she was new to the game and followed her movements with considerable interest. When she dropped a plate and the gulpers guffawed, Endite's glance showed a look of compassion. It was not Endite's habit to eat at the hotel. He was eating there now out of sheer curiosity. He had come to find out if she merited the extravagant things he had heard of her.

She did. Most emphatically.

It was worth that extra two-bits for your food to be able to sit there and watch Taisy Aiken. Girls were scarce in Dry Bottom and

1

the regular one was off having a baby, which probably accounted for Taisy getting this job.

At the Hairpin House you ate 'family style'—all the food being placed on the one long table. It was a part of Taisy's regular work to fetch those things which were out of your reach, and this frequently brought her into unpleasant contact with the men's eyes and hands and with their rough brand of humor. No wonder, thought Endite, she looked so flustered. It took a bold front to handle this sort of custom.

Her mother might be a 'gal about town' and her father no better than a strung-up rustler, but Taisy Aiken had the look of quality. It pulled men into that room like flies.

Endite watched and continued to wonder.

Awkward she might be. And flushed and harried by that boisterous barrage of crude wit and horseplay, but there was something about her that made you tingle. Endite felt it. He was bothered by it. He was bothered to find she could affect him that way. It took a pretty fast stepper to get Endite bothered; he generally preferred a little dash of the Spanish. And it wasn't her looks because she wasn't really pretty. Attractive, yes, with her yellow-brown eyes framed by that red hair. But those eyes took up too much of her face and she had freckles under them like paint splashed there from a too-wet brush. She had an uptilted nose that would have spoiled her looks if nothing else had. She wasn't beautiful and she wasn't smart. A smart mind back of those too-big eyes would have known how to handle this bunch of cow wallopers. She was just a green kid from the back of beyond; embarrassed, bewildered, completely out of her element. But worth every word of the praise ascribed to her.

She was in Endite's judgment, anyway, and he sought to pin down the source of her witchery.

It wasn't her clothes or gestures. Both were rough, to him, distasteful. He didn't see how it could be her figure, though admitting its attraction if you cared for tomboy models, accepting leg and not much padding. Frank Endite liked his cattle finished out. Liked to find some meat on them and something to get hold of.

He grinned a little grin at that and pulled back his shoulders.

He had his place in this man's camp. It wasn't a thing to be thrown away for a couple of legs and a hank of hair. A man had to watch his appetites. This Aiken kid had something, but so had a heap of other skirts; and this one, just now, had the public eye, an extremely dubious advantage.

And then she was coming up to him as though caught by his glance, maybe hypnotized by it, pausing beside him with those harried eyes plainly wondering what this fellow would try.

Endite's smile was disarming. Ignoring the others, he removed his silk hat with grave courtesy. "Whatever's handiest, please," he murmured and saw a quick curiosity color her glance.

The blood came pounding into her cheeks and the big eyes struggled away from his, to come instantly back with a grateful glow. "You won't be wantin' that hash," she said. "You might like the salad—I fixed it myself." Embarrassment swayed the shape of her then and color flew into her cheeks again, and Endite said gravely:

"That'll be first rate, ma'am. I expect that salad will be just what I need."

She gave him a long fluttery glance, burst suddenly into motion, reaching across the man next on his right and snatching the dish from beneath the descent of another gent's spoon. She piled half its contents on Endite's plate and excitedly met his eyes, and was gone.

Endite took a deep breath and peered back into his plate ironically, ignoring the nudge of the next man's elbow. It was Rubelcaba sitting beside him, and Rubelcaba's voice that said, "Damn nice little filly, but watching her slinging them legs around don't help a man none to digest his vittles. They ought to have ugly gals working here—she's hard on old arteries."

Endite nodded and reached for the bread. All the while he was buttering it his mind stayed on her, considering the changing shades of expression he had seen on her face as she stood beside him. Rubelcaba was right. She was hard on a lot of things.

He wondered briefly about Rubelcaba. The man's interests included the Spanish Cross outfit, biggest cow spread in the Santa Cruz Valley. Hired a tough crew and kept them busy; and kept right on losing cattle, being in that respect no better off than his neighbors. He was a big rough block of a man, bigger even than big Jade Fiersen. Bitter and voluble about his losses, cursing Texans and rustlers without partiality. "And why not?" he would say. "Ain't they one and the same? A thievin' outfit, and the way to get rid of them's to hang every one of 'em!" He had hanged two or three but he still lost cattle. What had roused Endite's wonder was the man's presence here when report had him off on a trip to Socorro. Endite reckoned that was a ruse put out for cow thieves.

Not that Frank gave a damn. He was a deal more pleasured watching Taisy Aiken as she franticked around the importunate table. Flustered and funny, she certainly was, but looked to be getting considerable work done and no one was kept any great while waiting—not that anyone would really have minded. It was a treat to watch her and their eyes missed nothing.

Several times during lulls Endite discovered her watching *him*. Whenever he looked up and caught her glance he could see the quick color climb into her cheeks. He wished he could think what it was this girl had, what thing or quality made him so aware of her. Many he had known more comely than she, but none had ever before so taken hold of him.

He attacked his salad with a scowl, ignoring her.

He'd keep his eyes off her. He was no

crass kid to be thrown off his feed by a pair of long legs and the shake of a skirt. He was calm Frank Endite, head barman at the Sparrowhawk, a man who knew his pasteboards and could deal a little faro between the whisky sours. *The* Frank Endite—one of your real high rollers to be named in the same breath with Dick Clark and Hickok.

He would tend to his eating. She was nothing to him. No female was going to change the pattern of *his* thinking. He had too much at stake to have it risked by a woman. A gambler's mind had to be on his business.

Let her choose up these cowhands.

Endite stared at her again; found that his glance had been expected and watched for. The shock of that knowledge slammed all the way through him. He glimpsed an eagerness in her, some reckless urge that reached out for him and rocked up through him like a jolt of red lightning. Her full sensuous lips broke into a smile, very quick, very brief, very startling to Endite. For with that smile she became something else. It was life she offered, lush, ripe and fruitful.

And, suddenly, Endite was no longer cool.

TWO

A NIGHT WIND came in with its smell off the river and Endite knew right then what he wanted. And also knew what he was going to do. He was going to have that girl and to hell with the consequence.

His first wild impulse had been to get up and get out of there, to fetch himself out of sight of that disturbing girl, and by that token, the reach of whatever the hell it was had got into him. But he knew himself too well for that. Getting away from her wouldn't solve anything. She would stick in his mind like a goddam burr. He must have her, know her, and then could forget her.

He smiled at himself and finished his salad.

Rubelcaba got up and tramped off with another man while Frank was pruning his stogie and lighting it. He sat awhile then, savoring the prospect, considering which approach would best serve his intention. Some females raised all manner of hell when they

8

found out a man was finished and done with them. This Aiken kid wouldn't be like that. She'd be crushed and quiet. He could handle her all right. She'd crawl off somewhere to lick her wounds. She'd be wanting to get as far from him as might be.

Most of the diners had got up and gone off while Endite smoked and looked over the angles. There were a couple of noisy drummers still eating and a brand inspector, come up from Tucson, was discussing the rustling with old Amos Tabbs who owned the Bar Triangle down near Tubac. Aside from these the long table was empty.

Taisy was busy gathering up dishes.

He knew she was watching him, sending quick looks at him whenever she thought his attention was elsewhere. He was glad he had changed his shirt before coming here. She'd be seeing him at his immaculate best. He knew he was the best looking man in Dry Bottom; looked and talked like a Princeton man and had the manners to perfect this impression.

He smoothed off the ash from his cheroot with a sigh and got up. Taisy was just coming back from the kitchen. The drummers had gone. Amos Tabbs and the brand man were scraping their chairs back. Endite eyed the girl. She stared back at him. Her lips showed her interest.

"Evenin', Frank," Amos Tabbs said. "How they goin'? Big game on tonight?"

Endite smothered his irritation. "Nothing special."

"You know Jim Tarlton? Jim's a brand inspector. We been talkin' about this goddam rustling. Getting so you can't leave a cow anyplace in this country without you put out half your crew to watch it. Half the riffraff from Texas has settled here."

Tarlton smiled, shaking hands with Endite. "Guess it ain't hurtin' your business, is it?"

Endite shrugged, wishing they'd shove off about their affairs. "Folks don't carve their names on a poker chip. Curly Bill's money spends the same as the next man's."

"Curly Bill!" Tabbs looked startled. "You think Curly Bill is behind this rustling?"

"Haven't thought much about it," said Endite indifferently. "Out of my line."

"Curly Bill wouldn't operate this far west. He's workin' that country round the Cherrycows—he wouldn't come way over here for his cattle." Just the same Tabbs looked worried. "You ain't seen him, have you?"

Endite said, more and more annoyed, "I wouldn't know Curly Bill if I bumped into him."

"Big heavy gent about six foot two with black curly hair and a freckled face," Tabbs explained. "Damn good lookin' and quick on the trigger."

"Then I haven't seen him. I would certainly know him from that description."

Tabbs peered at Endite somewhat suspiciously, but Tarlton laughed and allowed he didn't think Bill was behind this rustling. "Heap too busy snatchin' bullion from them chili eaters. Let's go outside if we're mullin' it over. Too stuffy in here—I'm an outdoors man."

"Good," Tabbs grunted. "You didn't hear about them cow thieves gettin' two of my boys did you, Frank? Filled—"

Endite smothered a groan. "After you," he growled, and held open the door. He hoped what was left of the outside light would show Taisy Aiken his handsome profile. As he followed the others he heard Taisy whisper: "Who is that man—that tall good-looking one?"

Endite tried to slow down for the answer. But old Tabbs was still running off at the mouth and so, reluctantly, Endite went after them.

He put his back to a post and looked out over the darkening river. Be a waste of breath telling these asses he was due at the Sparrowhawk. Tabbs knew better. The play never started before nine o'clock and it wasn't much more than seven-thirty now. He pretended to listen while he thought about Taisy. She had noticed him all right. *That tall, good-looking man!*

He wished old Tabbs would shut up and go home, but it didn't much seem like the old fool was going to. He had got off the rustlers. Gabbing about horses; Jack McCann's mare, the thoroughbred sprinter, Mollie McCarthy, that could outrun anything that ever wore hair. Endite looked at the river.

Most of the time, at this point, it was empty, which was how the town had got its name, but there was a good deal of water rushing north down it now. Endite suspected Nogales had been treated to a cloudburst. Some pretty dark clouds in the south toward the Border. Lightning made a considerable show there.

Here at Dry Bottom the sun was far down behind the western peaks and the desert soil made a pale buff blending with the dark-pooled shadows that lay under the tama-risks. Lights were beginning to spring up in the town, making a sleek oily gleam on the water. Heat of the day was diminishing now, shoved by the strengthening breeze from the south. Suppertime's smoke had quit the tin chimneys and more and more men were turning into the street, dust-powdered cow-hands and Mexican teamsters, with there and again the blanket-wrapped shape of some motionless Indian. Joe Cavanaugh came out of his store and stood on the porch with his hands in his pockets. Endite saw Michael Strawn roll by with a woman, and watched Rubelcaba go across to the Spar-rowhawk.

He shifted the slant of his shoulders im-patiently. He'd have to get away soon or it would be too late. Damn Tabbs anyway! He was like a kid with a rattle. There wasn't no end to his clatterous prattle.

Endite scowled, ground his teeth together. "You stayin' here tonight?" he broke into Tabbs' yammer.

"Well—" Tabbs said, and cast an eye at the lightning ripping through the dark piled-up clouds in the south. "Ain't quite de-cided, Frank. If that storm keeps up I might

13

have to stay here. There's a whole heap of water comin' outa them clouds."

"Lot of people in town tonight," Tarlton observed. "Where the hell do they come from?"

"Country's filling up," Tabbs said disgustedly. " 'Tain't like it used to be. I can remember this desert when there wasn't ten houses between Tubac an' Tucson. This wasn't no desert then. Plenty of trees an' grass—My Gawd!—the grass come over your stirrups! Not like it is now. If these wood cutters keep on like they're goin', in another ten years there won't be a tree in this whole damn country! An' there won't be no grass, no cattle or nothing."

He stared sourly at Endite. "You just wait an' you'll see. We don't git near the rain now that we used to. All these homesteaders coming in! And every damn puncher that kin save a year's pay wantin' to hit out an' start for hisself! Country's overgrazed now. What we need is more room, not more outfits. You mark my words, the free range is done for! In another ten years—"

Jim Tarlton said, "Let's let up on that before I bust down an' bawl. Who's that lean lanky hombre with that flossy dame— over there, just passing under that window?"

"Him? Mike Strawn, Fiersen's range boss. Ain't many of that crowd got the gall to come in here. Better keep away from him."

"Who's the girl?" Tarlton asked.

Tabbs spat disgustedly. "Nester's brat— name's Cherry Grant. Lives out to Fiersen's; got a shack to herself about two mile from the house. Old man was took with lead poisonin'. Fiersen let her stay on. She takes care of his place for him."

"Damn nice looker."

"You better lay off her. She's got one kid now they can't find a pappy for."

"Hmm," Tarlton said, and turned around to look after her.

"You better not let Mike Strawn see you doin' that. 'F he ever catches up with the father of that kid it will sure as hell be too bad for somebody!"

"That Fiersen crowd is getting pretty brash. Some pretty rough things bein' said in Tucson. He's been sellin' quite a passle of cow critters lately—"

"I don't wanta hear about it," Tabbs cut in.

"Rubelcaba," Tarlton mumbled, "has—"

"Lemme tell you something, Tarlton,"

Amos Tabbs growled breathily. "What Rubelcaba does an' says is Rubelcaba's own concern. He says a heap of things besides his prayers, but Fiersen's one galoot he don't talk about noways." Peering round he muttered, "Nor nobody else that's got a wheel in their think-box."

"He talked about him last week in Tucson, and anything he missed couldn't of been worth mentioning—"

"Never mind. I don't wanta hear it. I seen Fiersen kill one feller in this town. I—I guess I'll go home."

"What's your hurry. You folks around here is sure touchy about Fiersen. When the law—"

"What law?" Tabbs bellowed.

"We got law in Tucson—"

"Yeah. An' it stays there! All the law we got here comes out of a holster an' it comes a mite quicker for Fiersen than anyone! You better keep that in mind if you value your health."

Tarlton's grin was derisive.

"My health's just fine. For two cents I'd get myself made special deputy and run that gent in, just to show you. Cripes! Feller'd think you was talking about Curly Bill—"

"You better git yourself edge-u-cated!

Longside of Fiersen, Curly Bill ain't nothin'
but a two-bit amachure!"

Endite abruptly shoved away from his
post. "Guess I better be getting along."

"You an' me both!" Tabbs grunted, and
departed.

THREE

FOURTEEN HOURS OF saddle slicking had
brought Jade Fiersen back into the foothills.
And glad to be out of that dust and heat,
glad to be almost home once more, but no
sign of it softened the look of his features as
he followed the canyon's climbing tangents
into the cool clean gloom of the pines. He
was a good long way from being done with
this business—was beginning to doubt if
he'd ever be done with it. He had figured
for awhile it was chance that was shaping
things, but now he knew better. Remembering the rubbed-out trail of those cattle,
he had his own dark thoughts and did not
like them. There was no security left in this
valley.

Long acquaintance with trouble swung
him off the trail into the trees and he
threaded their brown matted aisles with cau-

tion. Near the far edge of timber he stopped his horse and went still in the saddle while all the restless force of his nature converged in that grim, long-held attention.

The sun was a dying blaze on the mountains and the trunks of the trees were black staffs against it, straight and bleak as the bars on a window, with everything else darkly steeped in its redness. Fiersen's glance, exploring mauve patches of the valley floor, found no movement; yet he was not satisfied, continuing his watch until the last lingering glow was gone. Then he turned with an irritable swing of the shoulders and put his horse to the steep-sided slope and rode up into the darkening hills.

In the brooding isolation of these uplands it was still, but he saw black wind-whipped clouds all across the south and could see the discharge of their downpouring waters in the continual flare of faraway lightning. Nogales and Tubac would be awash in that moisture and when it was gone there would be no trail for sharp eyes to follow. Not that it would have made much difference. Folks thought what they wanted to think and would be at no loss whom to blame for their troubles.

A smothered curse ripped out of him and

the highboned planes of his sun-darkened cheeks showed an edge of rebellion and then showed nothing, locking all away behind the inscrutability with which this man defied the world about him. But though he rode with a loose-muscled slackness, his glance was keen and his ears caught each sound that rummaged the quiet of this late summer evening. He considered these things for what they could tell him, and this care, this vigilance, remained unabated. It was a constant thing like the skreak of his gunbelt. The price Fiersen paid for continued living.

He stopped once in the brush by an isolated cabin and for several moments keened its unrelieved darkness, and then quit the road and got out of his saddle. Going into the cabin he said "Cherry!" sharply. There was the rasp of a match in that stealthy quiet and a brief glow illumined the shack's one window; then his broad shoulders squeezed through the door.

The dust-yellow road curled up through the hills and two miles farther on reached its end in a clearing backed against the fronts of three log-built buildings. Fiersen looked that way, then swung from the saddle and made a straight run for the place through the shadows.

A dog rushed out and he could see black shapes posted round the yard. There were no lights anyplace. At forty feet from the house a voice came out of the gallery gloom:

"That you, Jade?"

Fiersen said, "Who in hell did you think it was?" then sharply: "Where's Cherry, Slank?"

A shadow moved out of the ranch house doorway. Slank Calder, the Bar D foreman, grounded his rifle and replied in his half-amused negligent way, "Gone off to town. Strawn's with her—they went after grub. Bub's inside—hear 'im? Snorin' like we've not a care in the world."

Fiersen turned. Sent a gruff command rolling over the yard. "Take care of the horse, Joe, and fetch up the gray." Then he put his look back on Calder again.

"Not figurin' to go after 'em, are you?" Surprise was a sound in Calder's tone, not quite obscuring a plain disapproval. "Mike's been around. Probably knows what he's doin'."

"Mike's a hotheaded fool!"

"But of age," Calder said, and then came nearer and stood quite still watching Fiersen a moment. "You musta come onto somethin' didn't agree with you."

20

Fiersen waved it aside. "From here on out we'll be trading in Tucson. Bar D will stay plumb out of Dry Bottom."

One of the listening hands whistled. Slank Calder said softly, "Things have got bad as that, have they?" Then raised his voice. "Better saddle one for me, Joe."

Fiersen said, "Not necessary."

"But practical," Calder grinned. "If there's goin' to be fireworks I'd sure hate to miss 'em—been all of three weeks since I've been in a ruckus. What'd you find out, Jade?"

"Those cattle went over the Spanish Trail."

Calder breathed softly. One of the other boys said, "So it *is* Curly Bill!"

Fiersen shook his head. "I don't think so, Charlie. All I done was just follow the cattle. Till the sign petered out. They went out south of Tubac, then angled north. Near the pass they turned east. There was ten riders with them, really pushing them. Where they cut into the Spanish Trail the tracks was three days old."

Calder, twisting, peered into the south. "Time that quits there'll not be much left of it—the tracks, I mean. Storm will follow the mountains."

Fiersen silently nodded.

A hand came up leading two saddled horses.

Fiersen took the reins of the gray and mounted.

Calder climbed into the other one's saddle. A laugh came out of him. "Well, here's hopin'."

The man, Charlie, said: "Sure you don't want us to go along, boss?"

"You boys stay here and keep your eyes peeled for trouble."

He wheeled the gray and set off at a canter, Calder following.

FOUR

"CURLY BILL MAY be getting those cattle," Calder grumbled. "Or maybe the Clantons could be takin' them over after this bunch steals them."

"I don't see how they could change the brands—Bar D wouldn't cover any brand around here. It's got me beat—how do they get rid of them?"

"They've got a way, all right. Probably ain't botherin' with the brands at all. Might be shovin' them cattle clean through—"

"To the Animas Valley?"

"Why not? Old Man Clanton's got a spread in there."

"A damn long drive," Fiersen said, "and rough as a cob."

"Since when has a long rough drive bothered cow thieves? Curly Bill's got a place down that way, too. Might be they're both in it."

"Don't make sense," Fiersen said. "It don't take into account . . . Don't explain why Bar D's getting all the blame for this rustling. No Bar D man's ever been caught with a rustled hide. There ain't a single known cow thief camped in our bunkhouse."

"Well, they gotta blame someone," the foreman grumbled, and after that they rode awhile without talk, Fiersen studying the southern clouds. "Storm's coming closer."

"Goin' to foller the mountains; up this way before mornin', probably." Calder picked up the thread of his thought again, said quick and certain: "Be a damn good business—probably sellin' our stuff down in Mexico . . . Naco or Peña Blanca. Lot of damn funny lookin' brands around there. Could be unloadin' Mex beef up here—Douglas, maybe."

Fiersen said out of a long chunk of silence, "I don't think Curly Bill's mixed up in this."

"You can see somebody usin' that trail without cuttin' him in on it? You think he'd let fellers use a piece of his stompin' ground just for the hell of it?"

"We've got nothing to show it's going over that trail."

"Thought you said you'd tracked them onto it?"

"Yeah—*onto* it. That's where I lost them." Fiersen said reflectively, "One of Rubelcaba's riders chucked a shot at me this morning."

"Think he recognized you?"

"Quien sabe?" Fiersen sighed. "We used to be pretty good friends with that outfit. . . . Out in public, anyway."

"We used to be pretty good friends with a lot of folks." In the dark Calder's face shaped a twisted grin. "Looks like this range don't like us no more." He didn't sound very worried.

"Things are changing. In my father's time—"

"In your father's time," Calder said roughly, "there was a heap more grass and a lot less people. Your old man savvied what he was doin' when he squatted Bar D on

24

the best piece of foothills range in this country. Probably lookin' ahead to what we got right now."

"You reckon that's what's back of this?"

"You got this fight when you got these foothills; best graze an' best water. I ain't been ridin' this brush without hearin' things. It's a tolerable big country but it sure won't support all the outfits that's usin' it. Every time they look up at what we got, an' this drought an' all, kinda makes 'em see red. They tell me this grass used to reach to your stirrups—takes twenty acres to feed a cow now."

"More to it than that."

"Sure. A lot more. I been tellin' you, ain't I? Independence runs high on the hog, but a gripin' thought to them that ain't got it."

Fiersen took a look at him. "You figure I ought to let these outfits walk over me?"

"Can't see you doin' it," Calder chuckled.

"I'd give any man in this country his dues—"

"That ain't what they're lookin' for. Anyway," Calder opined in his hard brusque way, "we've give two or three of 'em all they had comin'." Then, amused, he said, "Don't add up to makin' them love us."

"I would never impose—"

"You ain't goin' to have to. That little ruckus in Dry Bottom took care of all that."

"You think I should have let that son of a bitch go?"

Calder said irritably, "You had him redhanded—Krantz deserved what he got. Aiken, likewise." He said after a moment, "You could of let the law handle it—"

"Blankenstraw!"

"Yeah . . . I know. But there it is, just the same. More of your high-handedness. Accordin' to local report, anyway. People don't like it. They don't like your eyes, don't cotton to your ways. They say you're too damn sudden with your gun—too final."

They rode several miles without further converse, Calder several times eying Jade, kind of speculative like, without opening his mouth. A man could see pretty good up close in this starlight. Seemed like Fiersen was turning it over, finding it hard to come at the right answer. Calder said abruptly, "Cat got your tongue?"

"What do you reckon I should do?"

"Hell! I don't know. Alls I know is that we're sure in a bind. Cows disappear, mostly other people's. That's one of the things that's flyin' round right now. Too many folks talkin'. An' when they get tired of talkin' ... Well, you figure it out."

"There'll be trouble, all right. If it's too rough for you—"

"I didn't say that." Calder gave him a narrowing glance. "You don't have to go more'n halfway to meet it." He said, kind of tossing it into the stillness, "Slack off a little."

"You can't fight fire that way. No, I'm not backing off. It wasn't us that hung Stack Aiken—"

"They say it was, an' most of 'em believe it."

"Other people have grass, and take care of their rights without turning the whole damn country against them!"

"Some gents," Calder said, "are born to trouble."

"I have never gone out of my way to hunt it."

"Nor gone an inch to one side to let it slip past you. They've got you pegged for a range rougher, Jade."

Half around in his saddle, Fiersen searched Calder's face. "What do they claim I've done that's so terrible?"

Calder stared between the ears of his horse, seemed to be listening to the clop of

27

its plodding, to the rhythmic skreak of the leathers, the tinkle of spur chains; and the smell of the river came faintly to him and touched his own wriggling moments of shadowy doubt. They were riding the dust of the valley road while the storm was rolling east through the mountains, away from this range like most of them did. You could see Dry Bottom's lights in the distance, a scattering of jewels on a velvet cloth. Tonight might tell, might forecast the whole grim, violent future of this country. Tonight . . .

Calder shrugged. "They claim you ain't co-operative. You don't drive no stock with the rest of these outfits; you wouldn't team up with that vigilante business. They claim you're slicker'n a hog on ice—that you ain't got no respect for the law. That feller Krantz is still in their craws; an' they're blamin' this blight of squatters on you. They figure, account of you lettin' them Grants have that shack it's brought in them others. They say it ain't natural, a cowman toleratin' nesters that way. Ain't a squatter in the country will say a word against you—an' that don't sit extra good on 'em either."

Slank Calder peered at Fiersen through the wavery gloom.

"Is that all?"

28

"No; them's some of the arguments. They don't like the way you look at a man. They don't care for the reps you send to their roundups—claim the only reason you send anybody is to spy out how many cows each spread's runnin'. Say they seldom turn up more'n a handful of ours, yet always you're shippin' out more critters than they are. More, they say, than you got any claim to."

"Talk!" Fiersen said with an edge of contempt.

"But where there's smoke you can bet there'll be fire. Them fellers ain't talkin' just to hear their heads rattle!"

"Most of that bunch got nothing inside to rattle."

"An' where will you be when some brash galoot calls you a cow thief right to your face?"

"They don't grow 'em that brash."

Calder wasn't convinced. "Once they get you on the run, you've had it, believe me. We ain't about big enough to take on—"

"I'm not going to make it any easier for them," Fiersen said with finality.

"If you ain't at Bar D you'll sure as hell lose it; an' if you are, by Gawd, them rannies'll hang you!"

"A pack of curs," Fiersen said. "It'll take more than that to get Bar D hogtied."

While he stared, those saturnine cheeks of Slank Calder finally ironed themselves out and he sighed without speaking. Ten minutes later they clattered across the loose planks of the bridge and came against the town's buildings. They walked their horses past the long-abandoned deputy's office and quartered ahead through the hoof-tracked dust that was yellow and mauve with the night's lights and shadows. And pushed on past the blacksmith shop with its smell of cold iron and stared ahead at the lines of hitched horses that showed solid ranks before the saloons. Fiersen picked out the Bar D wagon where it stood with its team by Ed Cantlicker's store; and he looked a long while at the girl on its seat.

"Town's damn quiet," Slank Calder said.

And that was when they heard the shot.

FIVE

"I GUESS YOU pride yourself on being a man without illusions."

Frank Endite had taken several steps and got into the gloom by the building's corner when the words came after him, nicely pitched to fetch a man up.

Endite stopped.

Tarlton said, "You'd know a good thing if you saw it, I reckon."

Endite held his place for a moment, then turned to peer into the porch's inky blackness. "Were you speaking to me?"

"I sure wasn't yammerin' at Tabbs," Tarlton said. "In a hurry, are you?"

Endite reluctantly turned back. "I am rather, yes."

"I won't keep you long. Got a little proposition I think may interest you."

"Yes?" Endite rubbed at his jaw.

"Step into the bar and I'll buy you a drink."

Endite wished he could see Tarlton's face. Why was he staying so deep in the shadows.

"Sorry. I never drink before hours, and I'm afraid—"

"Play don't start at your place before nine. You've got near a half hour."

"If you know my schedule better than I do—"

Tarlton chuckled. "That skirt'll keep. I'm talking money, and not the kind you put in a cookie jar." He thrust his thumbs in his galluses and watched Endite jovially. "What

31

I got in mind will put you on Easy Street. Move up here where you'll be outa sight. Now then," he said, and began to explain with his voice just a shade above the pitch of a whisper.

There was a lot more life on the dusty street when Endite left the Hairpin House and slipped through the shadows toward the Sparrowhawk's batwings. A girl came out of the darkness beside him, and he heard the sudden catch of her breath. "Oh, hello . . ." she gasped; and Frank peered at her dazedly. He didn't even think to remove his hat.

Someone pulled up a shade on the hotel's second floor and a shaft of yellow light struck across the road and imbued Taisy's hair with the shine of copper. She put a hand across her eyes and of a sudden she was trembling. "Do you—"

"Later!" Endite growled, and plunged on through the dust like he couldn't get shed of her quick enough. Yet on the Sparrowhawk's steps he paused to look back, heard Fiersen's name from a jaggle of drunk cowhands, and whirled on the instant to dive through the doors.

Like he'd looked on a ghost, he went back of the bar and broke out a bottle of private stock, poured himself a stiff glass and practically flung the stuff straight down his throat. About to put the bottle back, he caught sight of himself in the back bar mirror and went dead still, shocked by the haggard face staring back at him.

My God, he thought, *is that Frank Endite!*

He scrubbed a shaking hand across his face and peered at the Sparrowhawk's owner stupidly. Slocum came toward him. "What's the matter, Frank—sick?"

"Must be something I ate," Endite muttered. "God—" he said, "I got to get out of here," and brushed past Slocum with his knees like water and staggered into the man's back office, slammed the door shut and sagged against it, the breath sawing in and out of his throat.

You heard of guys practically paralyzed by fright but you never expected it to happen to you. You never thought it possible you could be so stupid.

He stumbled across the room, groping for the chair; collapsed into it with a groan. Drawing a strangled breath, he dug a finger around the inside of his collar. His head was hammering. He was shaking all over. Never in his life had he felt like this, and he

33

dragged a handkerchief out of his pocket and mopped it across his perspiring face.

If only he had not listened to Tarlton!

"God!" Endite groaned.

Someone rattled the doorknob and he nearly quit breathing.

The door opened then and Slocum stepped in, quietly closing it after him. He studied Frank silently. "You had bad news?"

Endite stared right through his boss. Mopping his face again, he shoved to a tottery stance and hovered there, handkerchief dangling from the limpness of his hand.

"Yeah—" He seemed to have to pull the words out of him. "Bad news," he said and groaned again.

"Mebbe you better take tonight off, Frank."

It seemed to take quite a while for Slocum's words to get through to him. Endite half turned then, feeling a blackness across his mind, feeling himself tremble, but reckoned—once he'd got this shock digested—he'd know what to do, be his own man again— Hell, that was crazy! Never in this world would he be his own man again. He was bought, stock and barrel. And would do what they told him . . . or one of these mornings he'd be found in some alley with his neck folded over a crate top and booted feet flopping from its bottom.

Slocum said again with his hand on the doorknob: "You better take the night off—"

"No—no, I'll be all right. Just give me ten minutes . . ."

"Take as long as you want. You'll be in no shape to deal cards, that's sure."

He went on out and Endite wiped his damp face again. He threw the limp handkerchief over in a corner and got a fresh bottle out of Slocum's desk. Breaking off its neck, he filled a dirty tumbler he found in the drawer and ten minutes later moved into the saloon.

Slocum sent him a slanchways stare. "You better tend bar—"

"I'm all right," Endite mumbled; and he did seem more like his usual self. The whisky was beginning to thaw him out. His cheeks didn't look quite as pasty now. He even managed a grin of sorts and clapped a hand on Slocum's shoulder as he headed for the gambling rigs.

This was Saturday night and the place was packed. Ranch hands bellied the bar three deep. There was a rowdy bunch of miners in the crowd, down from Helvetia and Greaterville to take a poke at the tiger, who might think it queer if Endite didn't take his chair at the table.

Anyway, he felt better now. The feel of Tarlton's money in his pocket no longer alarmed him like it had at first. Make no difference long's he kept his mouth shut; and even if he decided to renege on the deal it would take at least a week before the word got back and somebody set out to even the account. Plenty of time to buy a horse and get lost. If Tarlton had taken him a step or two farther—named names, for instance— But he hadn't gone deeper than the general idea. Too smart, of course, to give Frank the means of turning the tables. He could still go to . . . but knew he wasn't going to jump from the frying pan into the fire. Best bet, plainly, was to seek greener pastures. Plenty other places for a man of his talents. At Tombstone he could just about write his own ticket. Naco, maybe— get clean out of this country.

Rubelcaba crossed the room and Texas Crocket sent Endite a wave and Frank, distractedly nodding at acquaintances, threaded his way and found the chair at his table. Ed Creighton—he was case keeper—muttered something to him but Endite didn't catch it.

That bottle he'd sampled from Slocum's desk must have been private stock. The clamor that had gripped him didn't seem any longer to be quite as urgent; after all, who was Tarlton to be ordering him around. In this new-found euphoria he thought again of Taisy and wondered how she would be in bed.

Men came and loosely stood around his table. Talk sound flowed through the layered cigar smoke and rolled on past him, Frank's mind being turned inward; but he came out of this thinking to discover Rubelcaba and several other big ranchers making for Slocum's back office for their monthly session of high stakes poker. Saturday night at Dry Bottom and the crowd was flush and looking for action.

The betting started. Endite, warmly certain now, thought more and more strongly about Taisy Aiken, of the chance he had muffed out there on the street when she'd come up to him, ripe for attention. Maybe he should have taken Slocum at his word and sat this one out. He could have found some way . . . Hell, he'd eat there tomorrow and fix something—

Frank's glance suddenly sharpened on the board before him. Playing fifty-five cards instead of fifty-two could get a little sticky if some brash fool should back his memory against the visible evidence of Creighton's buttons.

There was quite a pile of money on the ten-spot; someone was betting forty dollars it would win. And it did win, too. And now the galoot's whole pile was on the ten, only this time the ten was being played to lose.

And it lost.

Endite, paying off, looked up to see who had been playing so smart at him. And suddenly froze, several chips falling out of his hand with a clatter. He was staring straight into the face of Mike Strawn!

"Well," the Bar D range boss said, "what's ailin' you? If your grip ain't big enough to hold them chips—"

"Sorry," Endite said, taking hold of himself. He picked up the chips and handed them to Strawn. "Sorry—my fault entirely."

The Bar D fire-eater considered him with a hard dislike. He counted the chips.

Endite lowered his eyes, tried to dissipate the emotions that were threatening to engulf him. What was Strawn up to? Why had he come here so close on the heels of Tarlton's proposition? Bar D usually did their playing at Kilpatrick's. Had word of Tarlton already leaked out?

To believe that didn't make a great deal of sense—even Frank could see that. No reason in the world why Tarlton speaking to Endite should have fetched Strawn down on him; how could Fiersen connect Jim Tarlton with this rustling? He'd better pull himself together, he thought, watching those hands put down their bets. But his mind continued to churn up questions, each new notion further undercutting the sorry state of his concentration.

He looked again at Strawn's face and then peered down at Strawn's hands, more and more convinced the man was here to take care of him.

Horror widened Frank's stare. Everything about him had that brittle, breathless look of strain as he watched Strawn's hands put that entire mountain of chips on the jack.

Strawn said, eyes bright, "I'm playin' that jack to win," and suddenly Endite understood too well. The *tell* cards in this deck were jacks and both of them were still in the box, the 'honest' jacks already gone. Strawn's glinting eyes told Frank he was aware of this. The man never glanced toward Creighton's case; his regard never moved from Endite's face.

Cold sweat came out on Endite's cheeks. He knew Buck Slocum, far too well to think his boss would let this pass. Slocum played all games to win.

Beneath his breath Frank Endite groaned; Strawn left him no real choice at all. There was a crooked jack four cards beneath. If Endite squeezed . . . Strawn would demand a count of the deck. If he let a tell-card jack come up the Bar D man would break the bank.

Frank Endite knew his time had come.

SIX

BISCUIT SHOOTING AT the Hairpin House—in Taisy Aiken's considered opinion—wasn't much of a way above just plain being an *abandoned woman,* and if there were a smidgin of choice in the matter she believed the abandoned ones had all the best of it. They had fine clothes, smart company to loll in, trinkets and jewels and good beds to sleep in; and some of the really high flyers even had their own stylish carriages to ride in. All Taisy got out of this deal was pots, pans and dirty dishes. And by the time she got a meal over and done with she guessed all the men who had been at the table knew as much about her as she did her ownself— or pretty dang near.

It just wasn't fair! Why, she might just as well be *purely wicked* and get a few pleasures along with the rest of it. She never had thought men could be so ornery!

She had just about reached the end of her rope when grub time came that Saturday evening. She had taken all the pawing she aimed to. When this bunch got out she was going to quit. Thirty-eight cents by the day, she thought, didn't even pay for the wear and tear. If this was the fruits of respectability, she reckoned she'd had about all she could stomach.

She didn't know how it was other places but life in this country was sure hard on a woman. And there wasn't but three choices open—only two, really, and maybe there wasn't but one, come right to it. Maybe there wasn't nothing but hell.

Of the choices, of course, the first one was marriage; married females said there wasn't nothing like it—that a girl never *lived* till she got herself married. But if you couldn't marry up with somebody, a girl

41

just naturally got nothing but hell, and of the two kinds available the working kind looked to kill you the quickest.

She was just about there in her thinking when she looked up and saw Frank Endite.

He was a tremendous surprise. Like a glimpse of the sun through the travails of darkness; pleasant reality after the nightmare.

Gawking, she couldn't hardly believe he was real, had never dreamed a man could be so beautiful. So distinguished and handsome it put a lump in her throat. So stylish! She had always reckoned those pictures in the catalogues were just made up out of people's heads. Like the pictures of horses; she had never supposed a man could *look* like that.

She wondered if he'd laugh at her like these others did. And that was when she dropped the plate and all those damn cowwallopers guffawed. She was so embarrassed she hoped to drop through the floor. Her face felt just like a prairie fire and she knew she must look a perfect ninny.

But *he* wasn't laughing—he even kind of seemed like he resented the rest of them. It gave her the queerest feeling. Nobody had ever took up for her before.

Then she thought how she must seem. Her hair was bound to be a fright—and all those skittish blushes! And dressed like she was with no decent clothes just old castaways and hand-me-downs that didn't even fit right; that only fit at all in the durndest places. And like her Maw always said, she was a heap too long in the flank for style. And skinny connected, and all those freckles! Fashionable ladies didn't have such blemishes; and he likely didn't know any female women but the very top bracket.

Because he was a kind-hearted gent and too polite to laugh at her sure wasn't no sign of anything else. Probably hadn't even noticed her— La-de-dah! she thought. What a foolishness!

He probably reckoned she was part of the sunset!

She dragged her look away from him and passed the spuds to Amos Tabbs before she noticed his own empty plate—made her feel plumb mortified.

With color pounding her cheeks again, she larruped into sudden motion, marched herself straight over there and pretty near swooned when Endite smiled up at her. He even took his hat off!

His voice was sheerest music. "Whatever's

handiest, thank you." It purely made her glow all over.

"Well, you won't be wantin' that hash," she gulped. "You might like the salad—I fixed it myself."

She was used to having men's eyes staring at her. Blue eyes, gray eyes, green eyes, black—they came in all colors and shades of boldness. Young eyes and old eyes, bright ones and rheumy ones; and she allowed there was aplenty ogling her now; but held by the stranger's upturned face she saw no other eyes but his. Then confusion swept her and her cheeks turned hot as the kitchen stove. Gosh, but he was beautiful!

He said, "That will be first rate, ma'am. I expect that salad will be just about right," and she jumped to fetch it, snatching it indignantly away from another and heaping Frank's plate with it, wondering if she dared meet his glance again; and when she did it was just like she remembered, gravely smiling, direct and *interested*. She had never felt so important in all her life.

Then she recollected all those watching cow hands and, with her cheeks fire hot, whisked away to the kitchen.

She was quickly back, flying around to wait on this man and that, taking care of them all with a surehanded energy, and making little chances to flash fleeting looks at the object of her daydreams.

When his glance was elsewhere she would study him furtively, admiring his expensive, well-fitting clothes, his eating manners, and the courteous way he conversed with that big ungainly Rubelcaba ox.

Once, glancing up, Frank caught her eyeing him and she blushed clean into the roots of her hair. But he took no offense, seeming pleased by it rather, and the way he smiled made her skin all tingly; and then a terrible thought crossed her mind. Supposing this fellow was just passing through! Waiting, maybe, for the nine o'clock stage!

It plumb scared her—it purely did. Made her knees all trembly just to think of such a thing. Probably headed for Tucson. Of *course* he was! What was there here for a man of his perfections?

She was glad this crowd was getting through with their eating. Some of them had already got up and she wished the rest of them would get a move on. She needed time to think. She wanted . . . Gosh, she thought, there must be *some* way to keep him.

She could scarcely breathe. She didn't *want* him to go . . .

There! He was pushing his chair back. Tabbs was too, and that tall galoot from Tucson was heading over toward them. Now they were talking; he'd forgotten all about her.

He was going to take that stage—she just knew he was. Going out of her life, and, suddenly, that life seemed unbearably hateful. She heard the tall man say, "Let's go outside if we're going to gab," and they all moved off, heading for the porch.

Taisy's heart seemed to shake every rib in her body. The cook came out to help with clearing off the table and she caught his arm. "Who is that man—that well-dressed, good-looking one?"

"Him? Frank Endite, the gambler. Don't have no truck with him."

But Taisy wasn't listening; she was thinking how handsome Frank Endite looked, how entrancing "Just like young Lochinvar," she thought, suddenly trembling. Crissy Bridwell, the neighbor girl back at the ranch, had told her about young Lochinvar once. Crissy had gone off to school in the East—she knew everything.

Frank Endite.

That was his name. Frank Endite. A gambler!

No wonder, she thought, he had looked so important. Surely gamblers were important people—like bankers and sheriffs. It took real work and study, a lot of *courage* to become a gambler. Any fool could start a bank. Any galoot with pull could get to be a sheriff—but *gamblers!* A big-time gambler was an act of God!

Taisy drew a deep breath. Made her feel plumb hollow. Her legs felt like they was melting right under her. Lordy! Frank Endite would be having little time for the likes of *her*.

Then she remembered his smile and in some way that helped. He wouldn't have smiled if he hadn't thought well of her—he had smiled right *at* her, and right friendly, too. Maybe . . .

She hurried to help Cook clean off the table. She rolled up her sleeves and got after the dishes like they couldn't be done fast enough. Cook eyed her quizzically, grinning to himself. But kept his mouth shut; he had already warned her. If she wanted to get burnt it was no skin off *his* nose. Grabbing up a towel, he pitched in to help her.

At last things were done and she was

through for the night. She was usually by this time plain dogtired and glad enough to drag upstairs to her straw-filled mattress under the eaves—but not tonight. She could no more have slept than she could fly from the rooftops. She lighted her candle and stood looking into the cracked mirror hung over the washstand.

Anyway, he had smiled. And he wasn't the kind to do that to everyone!

She remembered the clean white shine of his teeth, and picked up the chipped crockery pitcher and poured the basin half full of water. She scowled at the dust ring around its edge, wondering if things got all dusty in Tucson. She had scrubbed that basin out only this morning. She lifted it carefully down onto the floor; yanking the blanket from the bed she draped it over the window. Then she flung off her clothes and stepped into the basin. She was going to see Frank Endite again—even if it killed her.

She'd no idea how this was to be managed, but there must be a way. That stage didn't leave until nine o'clock. A lot could happen between now and then. If there was no other way she'd get on that stage with him—he might even ask her to go along with him! She purely hoped so.

48

She reckoned she must be a pretty bold piece.

But a girl never got nowhere being prim. She had lived around men long enough to learn that. They never wasted their money on wall flowers. A man liked to get a little action for his money.

Glancing down at her legs, she blushed, hurriedly drying herself.

Frank was a faro dealer. Faro was a gentleman's game. Only the real high-rollers dealt faro. Wheel men were held a poor second in the social scale; poker players and monte dealers were just plain riffraff. Tinhorns crouched on the brink of iniquity.

She had pretty nice ankles. If only she had something stylish to wear . . . . She frowned at the carpetless boards of the floor and remembered the lieutenant's young wife in Number 7 as she pulled on her ugly duds again. She guessed they would be out to Gilchrist's ranch; hadn't she heard the lieutenant mention it only this noon? Asking Jim Nolan where he could rent a carriage? If they'd really gone . . . If they hadn't got back . . .

Feeling purely wicked, Taisy slipped off her shoes. In her stocking feet, she stole to the door. Opening it quietly, she took a hurried look up and down the dusky hall.

No one in sight.

With pounding heart, she crouched outside the closed door and listened.

No snores or talk, except what was coming up from the bar. She stood pale and trembly, hearing the voice of her conscience scolding. But her heart wasn't pounding her ribs any more. It was scairt plumb still.

What she proposed was a terrible thing. Probably she would burn in hell for it.

But thinking she was likely due to burn anyway, she twisted the doorknob and found it locked.

She almost sobbed with frustration. All this bother and nothing to come of it! To be cheated like that right on the brink of success . . . Suddenly tense with remembrance, she flew back to her own room.

She got her key and came tiptoeing back. Her heart was banging loud enough now. She could hardly fit the key in the lock her hands were shaking so. But, there, it was in! She twisted the knob.

The door swung open with a drawn-out skreak.

A man turned over on the bed and groaned.

Taisy mighty near screamed. Only just in time she caught a hand to her mouth and crouched there staring with unbelieving eyes. It was a man all right—it purely was.

He lay breathing heavily in the middle of the bed with one knee pulled up, slack jawed, mouth open. Fully dressed. But it wasn't the lieutenant.

With a stifled gasp, Taisy looked at the door. The number wasn't 7 but 5. She could have wept with chagrin. And after all that risk. Even God was against her!

But she couldn't quit now.

Backing into the hall, she pulled the door to quietly. And backed right into something soft that yielded.

She loosed a shuddery sigh. She had backed right into a man's waiting arms; could feel his breath on the back of her neck.

There wasn't no use to think about running. He would catch her up before she took two steps.

"Well!" she said, and waited.

"What do you think you're doin' in there?"

It was old Mr. Gooms, the desk clerk.

"Lord!" Taisy cried, "but you give me a turn!" She twisted round, got her back to

51

the door. Then, born of her need, glib words poured out of her. "You should of heard—I thought somebody was murderin' him right in his bed—"

"Murderin'!" Gooms sounded startled.

"He's all right," she cried, "but if you'd heard that yell . . ."

Gooms said, "What's the matter with him?" and reached out a hand as though to look for himself.

Taisy said hastily, "Guess he must've been dreamin'. Or drunk; you know—sleepin' it off. My father sometimes used to do that."

Gooms opened the door, got the hall lamp from its bracket and lit it. He carried it into the room and stood with it over the man on the bed. The fellow was muttering now, though not so plain you could make much out of it. Taisy wished he would groan again.

Gooms, presently straightening, came out in the hall, put the lamp in its bracket and scowled around fiercely. Then he pulled the door shut, dropped the key in his pocket. "Drunk as a Hottentot. Lucky fer you he didn't wake up. You better hike back to bed."

He regarded Taisy unfavorably. "I'm surprised at you, goin' into a man's room like that."

"Well, but—"

"Yes, yes—I know; you told me. Females ain't supposed to think, nor go rovin' these halls in the dark o' night."

Starting to leave, Gooms paused and swung around. Gave her a dragged-out fishbelly stare. "I'm goin' to have to report this. If anythin's missing, cash money or trinkets—"

"Oh!" Taisy cried, and thought she must surely swoon this time. She picked up her skirts and ran back to her room. Flinging the door shut, she sagged against it, unstrung and trembling. She'd *have* to quit now—she purely would. When Mr. Gooms got done flapping his jaw about finding her coming out of that room she'd be lucky if she didn't wind up tarred and feathered. Plumb alone in his room with a strange man at night—lordy, lordy! How those tongues would wag tomorrow!

Taisy drew a shaky breath. She'd little enough time and none to lose if she would catch up with Frank before that stage left. It was now or never.

With her face pale as ashes, heart flip-flopping against her ribs, Taisy cracked her door just enough to see how the land lay. The lamp still burned. The hall was empty.

She was about to fare forth when she recalled that her key was in Gooms' pocket.

"Dreary me!" Taisy moaned. She would have to do something if she meant to see Frank; and this was the need that put her in motion. Down the hall she went, and this time made sure she was at the right door. Locked, of course; but she tried it anyway and, surprisingly, it opened.

With racing heart she stepped inside, hurriedly closing the door behind her. The room faced the street and was much lighter than her own. A trunk with closed lid was by the foot of the bed but Taisy, ignoring it, opened the closet to stare in amazement at the hung-up gowns of the lieutenant's lady. Not stopping to pick and choose among such an abundance, she scooped up an armful and spun to the door, pausing with ear pressed close to the crack. The pound of her heart would have drowned wild horses. She slipped into the hall with a silent prayer and, though expecting any moment a hand on her shoulder, got back to her own room without mishap. She tossed the clothes on the bed, shoved a chair beneath the doorknob.

She dared not glance at her face in the mirror. Dared not pause to catch her breath, even. This was no time to dawdle. It were best to be long miles away when the lieutenant and his lady returned to find their room burgled. Mr. Gooms might be summoned and all would be out.

She must be gone. She must be on that stage, on that stage bound for Tucson. She went through her loot in a frenzy of haste. Her trembly fingers couldn't move fast enough, couldn't keep pace with her flying thoughts. Oh God, she prayed, let me get away—don't make them catch me!

She had two dresses to choose from and a passle of underthings. Lordy, Lordy! All silks and lace—it fair gave her a turn just to feel of those things. The whole town would be talking; ears would wag and tongues would clatter. She got out of her own poor threadbare things in a rash of anxiety lest those people return and catch her still dressing. One good thing—she and his lady were about of a size. She was longer in the shank and somewhat less meaty, but reckoned she could make do—however the fit, they would be an improvement.

Just like her father! Thieving run in that family—oh, how they'd talk! But all she wanted was to get away. Please, God, she prayed, help me get on that stage.

Lordy, lordy! Did a lady have to scramble into all this stuff? Which went on first? Did you fasten this thing in the front or the back? What if you had to get out of it quick? Oh, the humiliation should she chance to be caught!

Taisy groaned as she struggled with drawstrings and gatherings. Imagine having to wear a thing like that—crushing yourself all up to nothing!

She thought she would never get her poor shaking feet down into the frilly legs of those drawers; but she did. Pulling them up with her cheeks gone scarlet, she hastily pawed through the rest for stockings, discovering she had come off without them.

But there was no time now.

She pulled on the blue dress. It was palely beautiful. Tugging it over her head, she was frantic she would tear it, so fragile it looked, so thin—like a spiderweb. It fit mighty close at the neck and shoulders, but not near so good at the waist as it should have; she guessed Mrs. Lieutenant didn't have no more waist than a hornet.

Lord it was scrumptious!

She tugged and patted and smoothed it down, wishing it weren't quite so snug at the shoulders; she felt plumb naked the way it made her stick out. But she hadn't the time to get into the other one—where were the shoes? Durned if she hadn't forgotten them, too! And the hat—ladies always wore hats. And always their hands were stuffed into gloves, too . . . She would have to go back—she would have to go back to that room if it killed her.

She was shaking all over as she opened the door. She was sure her heart would burst plumb out of her.

Like a wraith she crept down the dim-lit hall. What if Mrs. Lieutenant didn't have but one hat—the one she'd got with her? Or but one pair of shoes! Please God, she prayed. You been awful good about this so far. I can do without gloves—without stockings, even. But I got to have shoes. And a hat. Amen.

She pushed open the unlocked door, not stopping to close it. She went straight to the closet and felt around, but there was nothing on the floor, nothing there except a vague gleam of crockery. She whirled back to the closet. Yes, there was a shelf. And, glory of glories, when she stood on tiptoes her reaching hand found a whole line of shoes. She counted three pairs and wondered why in the world anyone would want that many.

She hauled down a pair and squeezed her feet into them, but she still hadn't found any hat or gloves. Her despairing gaze swept over the room.

Lights from the street showed a fancy box on a table near the window. Taisy ran over and snatched it up, shaking it. Didn't weigh any more than a couple of gnat wings but she could hear something soft sloshing around as she shook it. In a sweat she searched for a lock but all she found was a little flat hook caught round a peg. Unfastening it quickly, she lifted the cover.

There were two hats inside, both small, and a half veil looked to be fixed onto the top one, a pearl gray affair with a wide black ribbon flashed about the crown. Grabbing it up, she fled back to her room, not daring to stay longer even for the gloves.

She combed out her hair with flying fingers. Brushed it vigorously and caught up the hat and, with it, ran over and peered into the mirror, scarcely believing what her own eyes told her. She flung a quick look around but there was no one else.

She put on the hat the way the lieutenant's wife wore it, stepped back a bit and scared eyes searched the girl in the glass. Was this really the horse thief's daughter, Taisy Aiken?

Lordy, lordy!

She whirled away from the glass with flaming cheeks, put her head out the door, and cast a speculative look down the lamplit hall. Cold chills prickled the back of her neck as she envisioned herself passing Gooms at the desk. She was hot with a fever of impatience to be gone yet hardly dared take the first brash step that would leave her at the mercy of the first man who spied her. Suppose she met the lieutenant coming up the stairs—or his lady!

Be just too cruel! To be exposed, denounced, after all she'd been through—why, they might even drag her off to jail!

Her cheeks went pale. Her breath was a lump in her throat and she shuddered. She almost gave the whole project up, but could not throw this chance away. Hauling back her head, she softly closed the door; went and got the chair and wedged it under the knob. She remembered then the money she had saved—three whole dollars knotted into a handkerchief hidden in the mattress. She went back and got it, stuffed it down between her breasts.

She took the blanket off the window, quickly tore it into strips which she joined to make a rope and stood a moment thinking. Then she blew out the lamp, went back and peered out.

At the back of the house the room's single window faced on the river and she could smell the river's damp, strong and pungent in the dark of this night.

The bank below sloped steeply to the water's edge. She could not see that far, but from all the hopeless times she had stood looking out, memory flashed upon the screen of her mind the rough narrow path flanking the river's edge, and the willows rising darkly.

She guessed, by grab, it was neck meat or nothing and fastened her rope to one of the bed legs, tossing the limp rest of it out of the window, hearing it slither down the clapboarded wall. Heaving a sigh that was more than half groan, she clambered over the dust-gritty sill and prayerfully began her desperate descent.

Her wrists felt just about ready to snap off. She thought her shoulders would pull from their sockets. God, she gasped, don't let me fall!

She wished she had put more knots in

her rope—you could hardly keep hold of this slippery stuff; she couldn't get a grip with her feet at all and clenched her hands hard as ever she might but this hardly slowed the awful speed of her descent as the cloth seemed to fly through her burning fingers.

She could feel herself dropping straight down through space, the slap of the branches going past. Then all the breath was jounced clean out of her.

SEVEN

SHE LAY WITHOUT movement. This did not astonish her for how, indeed, could she move when she knew she was dead? She wondered what sort of funeral they'd give her. Nothing elaborate. Dry Bottom's merchants were long on cheap.

Suddenly she realized her left leg was hurting.

Broken, of course—bound to be. Still, it struck her as odd she'd be remembering pain, or feeling any, either. She'd never imagined a body hurt after death. She had never believed you felt anything.

She touched the leg gingerly. Broken, all right; it was all over blood. The stickiness of it was there on her fingers. Bone was probably sticking right out of it . . . . Hmmph—didn't seem to be. She thought of Stack Aiken, wondering if his neck had ached after they'd buried him.

Lordy, lordy!

And him her own blood father!

But old Stack wouldn't care—he never cared about anything. Aiken, they'd tell you, was any man's who would prime him. Just give him a good shot of redeye, hand him a rope or a running iron, and Stack was all set till the booze gave out. Everyone knew it. Everyone knew them Aikens was trash— lookit that young'un! Never more than half dressed . . .

It was thought of the dress that jerked Taisy's eyes open.

Lordy, lordy!

She was right on the edge of that drop to the river!

She forgot all about having broken her leg in her scrambling haste to get away from that bank edge—forgot the dress, too. Not till her back felt the hotel wall did she snatch any time to be thinking of anything. It was just after this she reluctantly reckoned she was still among the quick. Then she remembered Frank Endite and the nine o'clock stage.

Lordy, lordy!

She guessed she'd better get a wiggle on.

She'd no idea where to look for Frank Endite unless it would be in one of the saloons. And she would sure look a fright barging into a saloon in this get-up; ladies weren't supposed to be in saloons noways. Course, if she could keep out of sight until the stage was about to set off for Tucson she could clamber aboard and . . . "Oh, I've forgot my money!" she could say to Frank then, and he'd pay her fare—of course he would! When his eyes took in the way she looked in this borrowed finery he would likely be glad to pay her fare clean to Frisco.

Taisy sighed. Kind of wistful, she reckoned if he didn't she could always dig out her three hoarded dollars and go however far that might take her. One thing for sure. She daren't stay around here.

Might be better if she got aboard the stage now. Probably be smartest. The stage right now would be down at Riggs' livery. Ten minutes to nine Riggs would lead out fresh horses, then the stage would wheel round and pull up with a flourish beside the Hairpin House porch. Be a powerful risk to try to board it there; that lieutenant might see her or, worse still, his lady. Taisy sure didn't hanker to get caught up in no to-do with them.

Picking up her skirts, she started around the hotel, extra careful to feel her way lest she do more damage than she already had. Dress was like to be dirty enough now. Holding up, she began vigorously to brush herself off, hoping the blood from her leg hadn't got on the skirt. It did seem better— her leg, that is. Maybe all she'd done was wrench it, likely scratched it up a little.

Probably be best if she kept all she could away from where any light would fall on her. Riggs' livery was down that alley just past the Sparrowhawk. She had got to be careful. The whole thing depended on her getting out of town.

She wished she knew what time it was.

Where the side of the hotel made its corner with the front, Taisy hung fire, nervous as a chipmunk. She was getting in a swivet with all that rode on this venture, facing the possibility of failure and with her heart banging around inside her like a fly in a bottle. Never had she been out on this street after dark. Everything seemed so strangely different, not at all like it looked with the sun beating down. A durn scary place, she allowed, beginning to tremble.

Lamplight gleamed butter-yellow through dust-fogged windows, whole pools of it lying in the road like honey, elongated bars of it patterning the planks of the spur-scarred walks and spilling in golden splinters through the hang tree's branches. Wagons and buckboards seemed to be racked everyplace and horses were all about, stamping and pawing, dancing around. A studhorse someplace loosed his wild challenge, and rows of hitched bangtails stood hip and hip before the gray fronts of the roundabout buildings.

She heard loud shouts and laughter. Three riders tore out of the valley dark, flinging a great shower of dust in their wake and yonder, off down there by the Aces Up, some man fired a pistol three times and shouted.

Taisy, shrunk against the wall, visibly shuddered. She had not thought to find the town like this. The noise and bustle confused and frightened her. Never had she thought of Dry Bottom as dangerous, but she hadn't before been out in it this late; it didn't seem at all like the drowsy daylight hours she remembered.

A chap-legged man with a highboned face

rounded out of the shadows an arm's length away and gave her a brief surprised look, and went on again, muttering.

Taisy allowed she had better be getting on down to Riggs' livery. Next feller might want to stop and chin awhile.

This side of the street, the hotel side, was mostly houses and shops and such-like. It was brighter and busier on the other side where the lamps and lanterns of the town's saloons threw their golden gleams half across the road. Distrustful of these shadows, she was highly reluctant to go any nearer that rowdy crowd laughing and talking as they cruised the far walk. Busting to get to Riggs' stable and crawl into that stage, she realized abruptly there were but two ways to get there and, all of a sudden, she was scared of both of them. Scared to sift through the piled-up shadows on this side, afraid to trust herself among those men on the other.

In a sweat of indecision, she saw Frank Endite coming toward her from the hotel porch.

Her heart thudded like a pullet about to get its neck wrung. She felt shaky in the knees, for now that he was approaching what in the world could she say to him? This was something she'd not considered before.

Surely he'd speak to her . . . It never entered her head that Frank might not know her in this alien get-up. All of her worries were for what he might think, accosting him this way at night on the street. Suppose he thought her too bold?

With throat gone dry as the road's scuffed dust, Taisy moved onto the walk and went toward him.

A shade went up on the hotel's second floor and lamplight struck down, blinding her. She threw up a hand and found Endite beside her, and cried, "Oh, hello," at him breathlessly, and saw him pull to a sudden stop. He looked strange, almost haggard. He seemed hardly to notice her and she could hear the rasped sound of his breathing, almost like he was panting.

Taisy's legs went all trembly and, without knowing why, she felt suddenly frightened. Why was he looking at her that way? Almost as though he didn't see her at all, as though he peered *through* her, like all of his thinking was forty miles away.

She spoke, almost desperate: "Do you—"

He cried impatiently, "Later!" and brusquely shoved past her, breaking into a run that dodged him through a group of cantering horsebackers and fetched him, still running, to the steps of the Sparrowhawk.

With a gasp, Taisy turned completely around to stare after him, drained of all feeling save a blank astonishment; and then a voice said beside her:

"Hi, there, chicken. Don't that tinhorn like you?"

Taisy whirled, in a panic drawing back into the shadows, watching the man with wide-open eyes as he stepped after her. Dressed in the dusty garb of a cowhand, he scrubbed at his cheeks with a calloused hand while his eyes engulfed her, bright and hungry. His grin was unpleasant. "Ain't I good enough fer you?"

Taisy spun and ran blindly, wanting only to get away from him. She heard his boots pounding after her and changed direction, dashing out into the road and across it, toward the lighted fronts of the town's saloons. But her stolen dress, or the street's deep dust, conspired to slow her. "Here— wait!" the man growled and she heard a sudden scared curse above her. From the corners of her eyes she saw a horse rear up, snorting, as the white-cheeked rider hauled him back on his haunches, narrowly avoiding running her down. But she did not stop—didn't even dodge aside, but ran doggedly on toward the light of the Sparrowhawk.

On its steps she had last seen Endite, and where Endite was there would be protection. She did not reason this out, she just knew instinctively. He was the only man who had ever taken up for her; since he'd done so once he would do it again.

It never once crossed her mind the handsome gambler had done nothing at all for her. He had not laughed—as others had—when she'd dropped that plate; in her naive thoughts that was taking up for her. He'd taken off his hat when he spoke to her—that elegant tile that was part of his distinguishment. Nobody'd ever done that before. In her fright and confusion, she was trying to catch up with Frank, ignoring the unfathomable change in his attitude.

Almost to the porch she tripped and fell sprawling in the dust of the road. Stifled, blinded in this cloying fog, she felt strong hands catch hold of her elbows and lift her bodily onto her feet. He was saying something to her. Too upset to catch the drift of it she struck out, panicked, when—one hand still holding her—he tried with the other to brush the dust off her.

She heard his grunt of surprise. "You devil!" she cried, and furiously opened her eyes.

Lordy, lordy!

She found herself staring at Burr Rubelcaba who was regarded by all hands to be about the biggest of the country's cattle kings, second only in rumored worth and importance to Clay Allison. Nobody to stomp your boot and yell boo at.

"Sho, now, ma'am, I allow you've cause to be some upset, but there ain't no call to be usin' your fists on—" He broke off, narrowing eyes regarding her intently, mouth partly open in the start of surprise.

As he stepped back, his face pulled smoothly together. Round it was, bold and lively of feature, parting now to show white teeth in a smile. "Better let me brush that dirt off you, ma'am—"

"I can brush myself!" Taisy cried, blushing hotly, and got right at it, hoping thus to hide her embarrassment. When she discovered the dress wasn't purely ruined, that it did not appear to be torn or snagged, her fetched-up glance found him thoughtfully sober.

She had hoped to find him gone clean away, but there he stood, hat in hand, still eyeing her. Bull strong he looked, and un-doubtedly was—even handsome in a dark, heavy way, and very sure of himself in his high-heeled boots with that heavy black car-tridge belt strapped round his middle. Not be too easy to guess his age but he looked like he might be at least thirty. She reck-oned she ought to say thanks for his trou-ble, but having had few occasions to show gratitude to anyone she had no idea how to go about it.

Allowing she likely ought to make a stab at it, she said, "Expect you've got some thanks comin'. I wouldn't be wantin' you should think I'm not grateful—"

"Shucks," Rubelcaba said, and laughed. "Pickin' you up was a downright pleasure. You looked to be lightin' out right smart—you get whatever it was you was after?" Then, before she could speak, he asked with a kind of concern in his manner, "Wasn't fixin' to catch that Tucson stage, was you?"

Gasping, Taisy slanched a look around wild-like, ran a few steps to the Sparrow-hawk's corner, there to send a disbelieving glance down the alley. The yard in front of the livery was empty!

She was like that, breathless, almost stunned by this discovery, when a gun's sharp crash shivered the Sparrowhawk's doors.

The following quiet was like the stillness of death.

The girl's stare, darkly questioning, sought the eyes of the ranchman.

Rubelcaba shrugged. "That'll be Frank Endite, like enough. He's been drink—"

With a strangled cry, Taisy dashed up the steps and batted the louvered doors with a shoulder.

EIGHT

FIERSEN LIFTED HIS horse to a headlong gallop.

Calder, racing beside him, said: "See them two by the steps of the Sparrowhawk? That's where the trouble is, inside that dive." Then he said, "The girl's goin' in," and his voice got excited. "Ain't that Rubelcaba with her?"

Fiersen gave no sign of hearing his foreman.

When they reached the saloon, he pulled up his horse and got out of the saddle. Tossing his reins at the smooth gleam of the tie-pole, he went up the steps, Slank Calder following. The sound of sharp voices and a woman's sobs came through slats of the doors as Fiersen pushed through them. All sound stopped abruptly as heads swung round and went still, eyes hardening.

Smell of burnt powder was pungent. The gambler, Frank Endite, was sprawled on the floor by an overturned table and the girl who had been on the steps was crouched by him with her arms tightly clamped around the swell of his shoulders, head hugged against her breast, crying. And just across the wreck of that table stood Michael Strawn, pistol in hand, the whole raw look of him bitterly saturnine.

The sum total of this town was written in that picture. The thought burned through Fiersen's mind like acid as his gaze swept the crowd ranged about them. This was one of those things he had hoped to avoid. He had wanted more time, hoping to discover what was behind the antagonism directed against him, this black hate he could feel like a cold wind across him. That wouldn't be possible now. Whoever was pushing this had got the ball rolling. They wanted him to run. To flush him out into the open, crowd him into rash action and keep on crowding till they got him outlawed, and then got him killed.

They were out for blood.

Didn't make sense, but he could see it plainly. There was to be no choice for Jade Fiersen, no quarter. A wolf's game.

So be it. Fiersen's stare winnowed down till he watched them through slits; they would find what kind of wolf they'd called up. In a hard bitter way, this suited him. He was angrily fed up with slinking and shuffling, with their back-biting tactics which had forced him to caution. He might not care for the brutality of action but the rage inside him demanded something to smash back at. They'd given the dog a bad name and now were avidly waiting for the kicked hound to earn it.

Fiersen nodded.

He made a tall burly shape in the shine from the lamps. Light struck the solid jut of his jaw and turned the jade eyes of him narrowly brighter. Temper lifted his chest and he showed his impatience.

"Well?" he said bleakly; and Strawn, his range boss, stepped back a little. No one else moved.

Strawn said, "I shot the bastard," and gave them back look for look with contempt. "Them as don't like it can pick up from there."

No one grasped at that challenge. Nobody spoke and nobody moved, but a wildness threaded this room with their thinking, and the writhing behind it was as plain to Fiersen as the moaning sound of that girl's stifled breathing. Hating and waiting, but the violence sang through their looks and was steadily mounting, building to the time Mike Strawn would make his move to get out.

All this Fiersen saw and watched them, inscrutable.

"How did it happen?"

"How does a tinhorn usually get shot?" Strawn laughed without mirth. "He was dealin' from a crooked box and discovered I was onto him. Had some extras—*tell cards*— mixed in the deck. I crowded the play till I had the deal figured. He was usin' jacks. When the honest ones was run out I dumped my whole pile down on the jack."

"And caught him?"

"Frank didn't have the guts. He brought up his tell card an' paid me off. I called him then an' he went for his gun—I oughta killed the damn puke."

The brand inspector, Tarlton, came forward a little through the men standing round him, looked at Fiersen and nodded. "Here's the deck," he said quietly. "No extra cards here. Care to count them?"

Strawn's shape tightened up. "You calling me a liar?"

Tarlton's cold eyes surveyed him. "Not callin' you anything. Count the deck for yourself if you're doubtin' my word."

"So I made a mistake." Strawn's raw-red cheeks turned furious. "You think I believe that?"

Tarlton shrugged.

But the Turkey Track boss, Cliff Vance, eyed the Bar D boss toughly. "Mistakes is gettin' to be a habit in some quarters!"

"Be sure you don't make one," Fiersen breathed. Said clearly then, "Maybe we better have a look at Frank if we're going to get all sweated up about it."

Strain ran through the group round the table. These men, turned uncertain, gave back reluctantly, opening a lane down which Fiersen walked while Calder thoughtfully remained by the door. In the thin taut quiet, you could hear each roweled strike of his heels, the floor groaning under his step as he moved. It was a cool unhurried progress watchfully followed by all those partisan eyes.

Stopped by the table, he looked down at the gambler, seeing the girl's white arms protectively tense round Frank's shoulders, through the tear-wet lashes her eyes staring up at him fiercely. "Don't you dare!—don't you dast touch him!"

Fiersen looked at her carefully. A door slammed somewhere at the back of the building, turning him completely still for a moment; then his glance, coming back to the girl, showed a clear interest, strong and frank and not concealed as his anger had been. He couldn't remember having seen her before and he found this strange in a town like Dry Bottom. Her clothes, though disheveled, appeared expensive; but her hands, he thought, had known a mort of dishwater and, since she wore no ring, he had his own private wonder but did not allow this to creep through his scrutiny.

There was something about this girl that bothered him. Even through those reddened eyes it got at him, unsettling him, briefly turning his mind away from the issue, the need to get Michael Strawn safely out of this place. And it wasn't just her tears. He didn't know what it was, didn't try to define it, but its influence was there, disturbing and rankling, making him loath to say what he had to. He was loath, in fact, to consider her at all in connection with a man he despised so thoroughly.

He felt the build up of pressure coming out of that watching crowd, weighing him, avidly seeking some weakness to fasten on. A man in his boots could not afford many choices. Could not afford sentiment. It pitched his tone unintentionally harsh when he growled, "If you'll get up out of that—"

"Keep back—keep away!" she cried up at him, desperate. Her brown eyes were nearly black with her fright. "Ain't you done enough now? Can't you let him die peaceful—"

"Die!" Strawn barked. "Hell, he ain't hurt! Alls I did was crease the bastard—"

"That man," Tarlton said, "will likely die before sunup."

"An' if he does," Vance added, "you better figger to go with him!" And somebody yelled from the back of the crowd, "Let's give 'em a dose of their own medicine, boys!" and the girl, clutching Endite, started crying again in a way that brought Fiersen's chin up sharply.

"Mike," he said, "if you're through playing round with that pistol we'll go home."

Every hard-eyed look in that room swung at him and Cliff Vance, suddenly brave with this backing, yelled, "You ain't runnin' this—" and stopped like that, stiff and still, because Fiersen's long stride was chopping the space down, bringing him over that floor like a wall-eyed steer with the look of his cheeks wholly, frighteningly, wicked.

But Vance stood his ground. Though pale about the mouth, his face stayed defiant. "You've stopped callin' the tune around here—you're through in this country an' it's time you woke up to it! You ain't dealin' with . . ."

His talk broke off like something he had caught in Fiersen's look had choked him. Staring through the quiet with jaw gone slack, his eyes got bulgy. "Wait—" he cried hoarsely, and dug for his pistol.

Fiersen knocked it out of his hand, grabbed Cliff Vance by his belt and shirtfront and threw him backwards into the crowd. Big Rubelcaba grinned by the bar; and then Vance was up on his feet again, shaking. And now he was coming, boring in with bull passion, wild at the way he had been humiliated.

Fiersen's swung fist took him high in the chest and knocked him down. Booted feet were pounding the outside walk but Fiersen swung no glance at the doors; Calder was there to take care of newcomers.

Above thinned lips, Fiersen looked at the crowd. The masks were off now and those tense watching shapes were like so many wolves with mouths curled back from their snarling teeth, wide-open eyes bright and hard and hating.

Fiersen stood and watched them a long hard moment while the cow boss, Vance, pulled himself off the floor again and Fiersen drearily thought how many past times he'd found himself facing this same kind of picture. And he glanced at the girl beyond the overturned table, still crouched over Endite, crooning to him, staring back at him from the depths of despair; observing how the little hat set off the glorious shine of her hair, its color in this lamplight bright as burnished copper. Then he grimly pulled big shoulders together and sent a last look toward the valley's biggest rancher, Burr Rubelcaba, where he stood against the bar.

"Call 'em off, Burr. Call off your dogs before this place is wrecked."

"They're not my dogs," Rubelcaba

smiled. "Not my place, either—I don't care what you do to it." Then his grin widened. "Always kinda figured you would come to no good end."

"Mite early yet for long range predictions."

"You better take a look at your hole-card, friend."

Something faintly cold ran along Fiersen's spine and he looked a little longer at the valley's richest cattleman before pulling his glance away to send it raking back over the shapes that were nearest, knowing he'd about reached the end of something. This piled-up tension was a thing that couldn't last; only the lack of a reckless leader held this crowd in their places.

"Well," he smiled, "you ready, Mike?" and someone loosed a shaky laugh. He saw then why Michael Strawn was still, why the Bar D boss had not answered. Strawn lay crumpled on the sawdust streaked floor. His hat was gone and one bright thread of scarlet was spreading from his hair and slowly inching across his temple. The man had been conked, knocked clean out cold.

Then the crowd moved in, shutting off his view of Strawn, Cliff Vance coming again before him, big-knuckled hands white clenched, eyes narrowed, brightly hating. He was, thought Fiersen grimly, considerably tougher than he appeared. And still unsatisfied. Cocked and whitely furious, he looked to be teetering on the brink of violence.

"C'mon, you rustler!" Vance shouted; but before he could land that drawn-back fist, Fiersen jerked his gun, slamming its bore hard against the man's belly. Vance's gray face became suddenly frightened as Fiersen, shoving him roughly into the crowd, strode in his wake and came beside Mike Strawn's sprawled shape. Staring over the shifting heads, he saw Rubelcaba still at the bar, still wearing that enigmatic smile; and it bothered him.

With his gun he drove Cliff Vance aside, forcing him into the crowd's near fringe. The shifting pressure veered at once, men closing in behind him, swiftly locking him tight in their circle. A fist came smashing in from the right and he let that blow slide off an arm. Someone grabbed from the left and he beat that man across the face with his gun and saw his shape wilt limply down. Passions commenced to boil and steam. From behind, hard fingers clawed for his neck; he shook them off, lowering his head.

Hands clutched him again and he struck one man in the teeth with his pistol, that man's wild shriek, sailing up, was lost in the gathering growl of the mob.

"Get back before I have to kill somebody!"

A fist struck flush against his jaw, half spinning him round; another banged into his chest with a jolt he could feel clean down to his bootsoles.

Fiersen refused to drop though his shirt was ripped half off him now and he was beginning to have trouble focusing. *Where the hell was Calder?* He had no time to look. A man's sweaty face belched hot breath at him and he struck that one, with his fist, in the stomach. Somebody caught Fiersen round the neck from behind and he smashed that arm with the barrel of his piece and kicked another fellow's legs from under him; then someone landed on Fiersen's back and he was unable to heave this party off. He whirled instead, swinging all the way round, and the man's flying feet cleared an eight-foot circle before the fellow's grip tore loose.

"Stand back!" Fiersen gasped, "back, by God, before I kill three-four of you!"

They could hardly doubt. With the blood rolling brightly off his chin, rage still twisting his battered features and the tatters of shirt still hanging from his belt, he presented a picture that gave them pause. Sullenly, reluctantly, they gave back a little. He could see their eyes going over the fallen and some of their faces turned a bit sick—but not Cliff Vance's nor Rubelcaba's. Over their heads, still against the bar, he saw the pleasure in Rubelcaba's cheeks.

"You ain't out of this yet," the big rancher jeered. "Told you to look at your hole card, didn't I?"

Suspicion suddenly turned Fiersen's head and he flung one look at the door and knew. Calder wasn't there anymore.

"What the hell are we waitin' for?" Vance yelled, and came slashing in with both arms swinging, and ran head-on into Fiersen's left fist. The sound was like a bat being split, and left Vance with his feet but half under him. Fiersen hit him once again and Vance went down with a crash and stayed there.

Fiersen, eyeing Rubelcaba, said, "Get that girl out of here!"

The ranchman stared a long couple of moments, shrugged, settling elbows more comfortably on the bar; then his look took on a pleased understanding and he came away, moving toward her.

Fiersen heard him speaking to her, heard her tight voice cry, "You—you *gunman!*" and had no doubt whom those words were thrown at. He watched the roundabout faces, waiting; saw the girl go out and hold back one of the batwings for Rubelcaba who was carrying Endite. Saw the blood-smeared cowman, Vance, climb stiffly onto his two propped hands and sway there, moaning, before pushing creakily onto his feet to stand there gingerly feeling his jaw with his eyes still stupid. Fiersen watched the man shake his shoulders together, and it was plain there wasn't much fight left in him.

"Now," Fiersen said, "I'm going to take Mike out of here," and raised the gun in his hand suggestively. "You can play this the hard way or let me go peaceable. The choice is yours."

He knew most of these men; and they knew him. And did just about what he'd reckoned they'd do. They looked at Cliff Vance. Fiersen did likewise, and said in that hateful leisurely drawl, "Since Burr's not here, I'm talkin' at you, Vance."

The man peered back at him, lamp shine coming off his eyes with a mean dark glitter; but he wasn't quite up to carrying it on. "Go to hell," he growled and, turning, lurched away through the silent crowd. But at the door Vance said over a shoulder: "When you leave this town don't come back."

NINE

RUBELCABA CARRIED THE wounded gambler through the door Taisy held open and then, less carefully, down the Sparrowhawk's steps to the street. When they reached the comparative gloom of the alley leading off toward Riggs' lantern-lit stable, he dropped Endite's feet and let him go sprawling. With a cry of concern, Taisy sprang to aid him but his inert weight proved too much for her slender strength. He slid from her support, took his fashionable clothes down into the dust where he lay, unmoving. Dropping beside him, Taisy lifted a stricken face to where Rubelcaba looked on with a lip curled. "Oh, please—" Taisy cried from the depths of despair. "Won't you be helpin' me fetch him to a doctor?"

The rancher's big shape stood a moment longer as though undecided. There was something about this burly fellow's stare, a kind of malicious indifference, that gave the impression he was not much concerned, now he had gotten Frank away from the saloon. Why this should be Taisy could not imagine; but she could not forget the heartless way he had dropped Frank, almost as though he were washing his hands of him, almost as though he'd found the contact distasteful.

And time was so precious!

That man—that tall one who'd counted the cards in there—had said Frank would like enough die before morning; the thought was a twisting knife in her heart. She felt weak as a katydid, shaking all over. She must be cool to think while there still was time to do something for poor Frank—he had to have help! There must be some way to reach this man; she could scarcely pull her thoughts together with poor Frank lying there groaning his life away.

She could only catch at Rubelcaba desperately. "Please—oh, *please!* Can't you help just a little? Can't you find Frank a doctor?"

"Doc Crailvine's office is just down there a ways—"

"But can't *you* help? There might be . . . Surely you wouldn't deny him that chance?"

Rubelcaba muttered something under his

breath, made a downswinging, irritable turn with his shoulders, reached down, caught Endite's arm and jerked him roughly to his feet. "Stand up there! Who the hell d'you figure you're foolin'?" He cuffed Frank's face with an open palm, stepped back away from him, watching him narrowly. "Fall down again and I'll kick your damn ribs in."

Endite swayed precariously, Taisy eyeing the rancher with indescribable horror. "You—you heartless beast!" She ran to the gambler, catching him, steadying him. "Oh, my dear! My poor dear!"

Rubelcaba's lip curled. He made one further effort to show her the truth of this, though she wasn't his problem and he was through with Endite. "He's wastin' your time—" he began, and shut his mouth. She wasn't hearing a word, too busy trying to keep Endite upright.

The rancher scowled at them, embarrassed to think she could be such a goose. Hell, she was asking for it! He gave a snort of disgust and said, wryly amused, "I expect he'll make it if you let him lean on you enough." Then he turned his back and walked off, forgetting them.

Cloaked by shadows, he considered the

Sparrowhawk. There should have been shots coming out of there by now. Were they going to let Fiersen bluff them out after all?

Rubelcaba had reached the saloon's spur-scarred steps when the cowman, Vance, shoved open the batwings and came heavily out. Rubelcaba took a look at the man's pounded face and beckoned him a little apart from the others who were now spilling into the street like whipped curs. "I dunno," Vance said with a still glazed stare. He gave a dubious headshake. "I dunno what went wrong . . . Might be if you had stayed a bit longer—"

Rubelcaba wasn't listening. He was bitterly considering how they'd been outsmarted. Been going slick as slobbers till Fiersen had yelled to get the girl outside. Rubelcaba hadn't aimed to oblige until it crossed his mind Fiersen wanted her out so he could unleash his artillery, which was why he had picked up Endite, knowing the girl wouldn't budge with the tinhorn left to bleed on that floor. Thanks to Tarlton she'd supposed the man dying; Rubelcaba by that time had reckoned Fiersen's finish could be safely left to this bungling Vance.

He slanched the man an intolerant glance. They'd had Fiersen trapped and this feather-witted cow walloper had let him get out of it. Now they had it all to do over!

Tarlton came down the Sparrowhawk's steps, drifting over to stand idly by while Vance fumed dire predictions and big Rubelcaba, still awash in the venom of disappointment, darkly scowled at the cloudblack peaks of the Ritas. Tarlton, following his look, saw how the storm was swinging around, running low across the eastern slopes, gathering speed and building fury which would spill too late to give this range any moisture. To have come so close! Rubelcaba thought turbulently. To have snagged his loop on these fools' stupidity!

All those weeks spent in readying the stage, all those months of furthering whispers, spreading their poison with subtle patience; all the sweat and the work; all the forty-eleven details he'd had to see to, the maneuvering and figuring—all of it lost because that damned Cliff Vance hadn't the wit to think for himself, couldn't act for once on his own initiative.

Rubelcaba swore under his breath. "What's that?" asked Tarlton, and Rubelcaba snorted. It was too late now to swing this around; he would have to set up something else. Fiersen, at least, was still in the saloon. He would still have to pack his range boss out of there and someway get the man down to the wagon where that unmarried mother . . . .

The rancher stiffened, but shook his head. He'd keep this in mind but tonight he had better let bad enough alone. His influence might not survive another fiasco. Give the man rope. That was the ticket. Give him more cattle. Hell, the way things were going—all a man needed was to be a little patient. Fiersen's own personality, his habits and brashness coupled with the stories of this night's work should prove his undoing before any great while.

Burr Rubelcaba took a grip on himself and said without rancor, "Guess this trick goes to Fiersen, boys. There'll be another time he won't ride so high. Fellers he used that pistol on ain't like to be forgettin' in no damn hurry."

"He's got guts," Vance muttered, and was jerked once more by his nerves and excitement, swinging into a restless tramping. Tarlton, eying Rubelcaba, said, "Where do we go from here—or don't we?"

"Expect we can leave the next move up to him."

"He ain't got many choices," Vance grumbled grimly. "Guess he knows what this country thinks of him now."

"The word'll get around," Tarlton nodded, "but names are a dime a dozen. Talk's cheap. You don't hang a man till you catch him at it. Fiersen's a pretty slick article."

Vance said doggedly: "You can't keep stealin' and not get caught. Sooner or later someone'll catch him."

"Think so?" growled Tarlton. "Nobody's got the goods on him yet."

"Nobody really suspected him till recent," Rubelcaba put in. "Hard to suspect one of your neighbors of swingin' a wide loop. Takes a bit of time for a thing like that to sink in. Like eatin' olives or love apples—takes a heap of samplin' for a feller to get used to 'em. Things'll move faster now it's out in the open. Folks'll be keepin' their eyes skinned now."

"If I seen him messin' with any cows of mine," Tarlton said, "I'd damn sure shoot first an' auger at him later."

Rubelcaba's thoughts, turned inward, went harking back to the recent fiasco. "One man," he muttered, "an' he made it stick."

WHEN he saw Rubelcaba stride away and desert them, Endite pulled away from the

92

girl and straightly stood upon his own two feet. "Trash!" he breathed in an affronted voice, then saw the girl's look and pulled himself together. But he could not seem to keep his back rightly stiff nor the sag entirely out of his shoulders. He made to move and staggered; with an obvious reluctance, he re-accepted her help. "If you'll just kind of steer me I expect I can manage."

"But—"

"There's nothing wrong with my legs," Endite grunted. "Rubelcaba was right—I'm not much hurt—nothing a little rest won't cure. Just a crease; I suppose it must have fractured a nerve. For a time, seems like, I just couldn't move."

"My poor dear," Taisy cried, squeezing his arm in a paroxysm of sympathy. "Do you think—"

"I'll be all right . . . A little faint, I guess, from the loss of blood—shock, perhaps. Probably wear away. Nothing for you to be upset about, ma'am. I've rooms down over the Chinese laundry . . . If you could steady me that far—"

"Of course I will. But you should be seeing a doctor, Frank. That man said—"

"Tarlton?" The name sounded harsh the way Endite said it. He pulled up the sag in his shoulders. "We'll make it, all right. Just keep hold of me."

"But . . . Oughtn't you let a doctor look at it?"

"My dear young lady—" Perhaps his breath, the energy it took to mount words on it, escalated the pain from his wound. Endite grimaced and suddenly turned his face away. "Miz Taisy, ma'am," he gasped without bringing his head around, "you shouldn't be seen with me—coming into that barroom was bad enough. The city fathers—not to mention their wives—would never condone your coming to my rooms. A card cheat—"

Taisy said indignantly, "But you *didn't* cheat! That man Tarlton . . ."

"I know, my dear. Give a dog a bad name and it's not easily forgotten. A gambler can't shrug off such talk. I will play no more cards in this town; I am through here."

"Never mind. We'll go someplace else."

Endite drew a sharp breath. He fetched his head round, then looked away to say, "More of life's little ironies. Bless you! That you should think of such a thing . . . I am prostrated, madam." He stared straight ahead of him into the dark. "It's too late for that; they've judged and found me short

94

measure. The evil that fellow has loosed will spread; his lie will color any pursuit I tackle. You must think of your reputation, Miz Taisy."

"Oh, la!" Taisy cried.

"Nevertheless," declared Endite, "I shall not permit you to risk it, ma'am. You behold in me a ruined man. All the scruples I have cultivated, those tenets of good conduct and fair dealing for which I have been known, the very virtues upon which my character has been erected—all these have been swept away and become as nothing. It's not enough that I've been vindicated; that before their very eyes that fellow from Tucson made the count and proved beyond dispute my honesty. Slander clings. I shall never permit you to share it, madam."

He could feel her peering up into his face and kept his own, jaws clamped, straight front. She said scarce above her breath: "I wouldn't be carin' about that, with you."

The tightness of Endite's grip suddenly hurt. He stood completely still. He loosed a sigh and said gruffly, "All right, you can help me. But only so far as the laundry, ma'am."

TEN

FIERSEN, HOISTING STRAWN'S slat-thin body across one shoulder, straightened up as the last of the cow crowd boomed their way down the Sparrowhawk's steps. Ignoring the stares of the loitering townsmen, he shifted Strawn's weight with a hard wrench of muscles and, face bleak, walked the length of the silent bar. There was nothing he could say to these scowling men; they'd judged him, condemned him and cast him out. Perhaps it was because of this there was no redeeming gentleness showing; at any rate, it was toughness and that cold unbending ignoring of obstacles which had carried him through the hate in this place.

On the porch's warped planking he stood a grim moment scanning the street, taking his feel of the town's pulse again. Fellow could learn a good deal if he kept his eyes open and could translate what they saw.

He watched the crowd breaking up into outfits, and saw Rubelcaba by the foot of the steps with Vance and that brand man from Tucson, Tarlton, the one who had counted the cards from the faro game. And now the man looked up with a slow lingering stare; the street turned quiet and Rubelcaba, displeased with this cessation of movement, threw a low harsh growled command at his crew. "Climb on—climb on! Let's get out of here!"

Fiersen watched them fade through the lemon fog, watched that drifting dust thin and settle. There were still too many men on this street. Most of these, though they might not look it, were sure to be keeping tabs on him, still dissatisfied, ready for trouble if only they could find one thin streak of softness to encourage their anger to tear loose again.

The mood of this town was still ugly. No one had changed his mind in the least. Cowed for the moment but they weren't forgetting. They still saw Fiersen as a goddam cowthief; you could feel that thinking chousing round inside them, feeding their venom, turning them bitter and wolfing them up again.

There was a weight in his fist, the one hanging at his side; and he lifted it up, sardonically discovering it still held the pistol. He put it away, eyeing Vance's pounded face in the light from a window. "Remember what I told you," Vance growled. "Don't come back."

Fiersen shifted Strawn's weight and got out the makings. There was no use in talk; he pitched them away and went down the splintery steps, brushing past Vance and that fellow from Tucson, observing Slank's horse was gone from the tie rail. He caught the reins of his own and was turning away when he saw Calder up the street by Mike's wagon. The man was talking with Cherry Grant on its seat. And it was plain by the way she sat the girl's attention was grudging, resentful. Seeing her that way made Fiersen darkly shake his head. He lowered Mike's body, led the horse toward the wagon.

He knew the girl wasn't looking for sympathy; seemed fiercely determined not to need anyone—least of all a man. Many times he had seen that indrawn expression, this blankness of countenance when Calder or Strawn made attempts to engage her. Strawn, Fiersen knew, was in love with her; he also knew how little she encouraged him, even less perhaps than she encouraged Slank Calder.

Everyone had their troubles, it seemed

like. And most of them stemmed from the spur of the moment. Man could do a mighty lot of fool things; and some of those things could not be repaired though a man gave up the rest of his life to it.

Feeling all the weight of his twenty-eight years, Fiersen sighed. But it wasn't the years that bothered him; just a handful of months that had gone into one of them when he'd been too young to know the meaning of restraint. Brush running months spent over in Texas, Panhandle mostly. It was all in his mind of course, and he knew this. The remembrance had been haunting Jade Fiersen for the last five years. It could wear a man out.

Fiersen's lips quirked a bit, wistfully, sadly. What a macho he'd been in those Texas months—a man among men, he'd thought at the time. Seeing his face on a handbill had tickled him; how proud he had been to ride with Jack Ketchum! He was not proud now but filled with regret for those ill-advised days, filled with disgust that he could have been such a fool.

Three months he had larruped, riding high with the wildest. Three months of excitement and high-handed deviltry; and, suddenly, there wasn't any fun left in it.

Wimpy's death had shown him the truth. Wimpy had been his saddle pard; young, reckless, always laughing, cutting capers. Wimpy's last caper had been that raid on the great Bell ranch; Wimpy's death had matured him overnight. Really Fiersen had been lucky; he'd never killed anyone up to that time but had seen right then what end he'd been heading for, and he'd determined to get plumb away from it, pronto. Yes, he had glimpsed the writing on the wall; some fine day they'd stop one train too many and a lot of those boys would be lying crumpled and broken along the right-of-way. Breed of the chaparral . . . He wanted no part of it.

Fiersen had hung and rattled for a while, hoping to talk Black Jack into quitting that life; but it hadn't worked out. Sam, Black Jack's brother, hadn't cottoned to breaking up the bunch. More than once Fiersen had seen that snaky glint in his eye. "Just one more haul," Jack had said.

Folsom Flagstop was the place they'd picked for it. They had taken a pasear up into New Mexico, thinking Folsom the best place to stop Conductor Harrington's train. A fine spot it looked, just outside town at the upper end of a long hard pull; they'd had it all doped out. "Be a cinch," Sam said; so they'd holed up a while, not anxious to try their luck when they'd have to pack grain to keep the horses in flesh. So they'd lazed around, playing cards, and one day the Ketchum brothers got into a row in which a lot of hard words were being flung about. The upshot was that Jack and Fiersen had quit the camp and took off on their backtrail, having finally seen the error of their ways.

But they had waited too long.

Happily unaware of the joker Fate was getting ready to slip into the deal, they'd cut off through the mountains to Tucumcari. "Six-Shooter Siding" the place was called then, and a wild place it was on the Rock Island Railroad. They'd stuck around a few days, gambling, trying to build up a stake of honest money. Then one night at the worst dive in town, the marshal had come in with another man back of him; and this man at once had cried out their names. Fiersen and Ketchum had grabbed out their irons, backing toward a cobwebbed window. Violence had been the farthest thing from their minds.

Fiersen had kept the crowd at bay while Ketchum got out through the window; the idea being that Jack, outside, would cover them for him. Before Ketchum's boots hit

the dirt outside, the man behind the marshal had flipped up a pistol. One of his
shots struck Fiersen high in the shoulder;
he'd fired back instinctively. Nausea maybe,
or perhaps the pain, had unsteadied his aim.
Through acrid smoke he'd seen the marshal
wilt into a table; the man who'd come with
him had been Jack's brother Sam.

They'd gotten clear, rode half the night,
Black Jack vowing he would pay off Sam if
it was the last thing he did. Said Jack,
"We'll stop Harrington's train ourselves—
tonight, by Gawd! Tomorrow night when
Sam's bunch figure to pull their coup them
coaches will be packed with railroad dicks!"

In vain Fiersen tried to talk him out of it.
Black Jack was adamant. He patched Fiersen
up, all the while ranting about Sam's treachery. Fiersen was too shook up to argue; he
kept seeing that marshal wilting into the
table. He was convinced right then he would
never get over it. What he hadn't known
then—nor Black Jack guessed, was that Sam
and the boys had already stopped Harrington. They found it out when they stopped
the train that night going north.

"You're in bad shape," Jack told Fiersen,
scowling. "You stick back in the brush and

hang onto the horses. I kin take care of this chore myself."

Puffing and panting, the train crawled up the grade. Jack had thrown some ties across the track. The engineer brought the train to a stop. Jack figured to have things well in hand when Conductor Harrington opened the mailcoach door and turned loose both barrels of a shotgun. Black Jack staggered back and went down. There hadn't been anything Fiersen could do; half the coaches had been filled with Pinkerton men and the track was a-crawl with them. He had been plumb lucky to get away and had stayed hidden out till he was able to travel.

The Santa Cruz valley had looked mighty good to him; he had learned his lesson and had since gone straight. Small wonder then if his thoughts were bitter at what he saw shaping up in this country.

He stared again at the girl in the wagon, and peered once more at Calder, still talking. Why couldn't people leave other folks alone? Why did they have to keep poking at things? What was wrong with this world that it should hold such a load of grief and unpleasantness? Was there no hitchrail of faith a man could tie onto?

He pulled his glance off them, unaccountably irritable. He'd no intention of handing out unwanted advice; what could he know of what went on in her head? He knew little enough of what notions shaped Calder— why hadn't Calder stayed put at that door?

He wished there was something he could do for the girl, something he could say that might help her; and this was his weakness, this compassion for others. Their hopes and desires, the little things which swayed them, were real to him. Out of his own experience they conjured bleak pictures.

Why did God put these burdens on people? On a fine girl like Cherry whose only mistake was to have loved an unworthy man too well. She tried to hide the misery and heartbreak . . . and that tall young girl who had cried for Frank Endite! There was ever this sharp regret in Fiersen . . . This was the softness which, if ever discovered, might one day kill him.

These were things he kept locked inside him. To these hipshot men, so furtively watching, he was a burly, bull-necked figure of a man with straw colored hair and highboned features that, habitually darkly taciturn, inscrutably matched the bleak look of his eyes, which were green and disconcertingly steady. He was a man with a will and that hard, sure way that spelled efficiency. You could feel that will like a physical impact, a curt reminder he had not been called 'Jade' for nothing.

Under the flail of that bright green glance, they fell grudgingly back and permitted him passage. And this was his power in that violent land. This certainty of immediate and implacable reprisal. Tales of this man's doings had furnished much material for after-supper yarning round the night fires of the cow camps. They said he never stepped out of his way to hunt trouble, nor swerved to avoid it—but they were wrong in that. He'd been trying to avoid it for five years now.

The whole town watched him pack Mike Strawn up the empty street to the Bar D wagon. Cliff Vance reckoned he used good judgment in not rousing his range boss before, at the wagon, making him as comfortable as might be. And maybe it was good judgment; Fiersen didn't need more trouble.

He watched Cherry Grant fetch her look around wonderingly when Strawn's inert weight thumped the wagon bed. She was a girl who hated violence. She took her pleasures, Fiersen thought, from life's quiet ways that others, more fortunately placed, found humdrum. He'd seen her watching the way of clouds and wind through a field, a rapt and mysterious light in her eyes; he'd observed her racing a shadow on horseback, riding free as a zephyr across the dun range. She could lose herself staring into the red heart of a campfire. These things he knew for he'd taken her camping. And now compassion softened the set of her features as she glanced at Strawn's shape.

"Is he hurt?"

"Got banged on the head—he'll get over it."

"A fight?"

He guessed what she was thinking and did not feel she required an answer.

"This town," Calder grinned, taking his knee off the horn, "is a heap inclined to dub Jade a rustler."

Her eyes grew dark as they inspected his face. Her glance swung to Fiersen and her thoughts changed the lines of her face at once, quite noticeably. And there was a change in her breathing. Calder's lips quirked.

She was not so tall as the girl who had cried over Endite, but more mature though about the same age, more composed, more graceful. Calder tried to get a look at her eyes but her face had gone into the shifting shadows. He watched how her hands went out and caught at the seat edge, and from that gesture drew his own conclusions.

Cherry said from the depths of her thinking, "When hate is let loose it grows and spreads like a creeping devil—not even the dirt of the grave can turn it. They hated my father when they rode out and killed him. His name is hated just as bad today and I suppose it will still inspire hate after I'm dead and they have buried my child." She stared at Fiersen. "Let them have this range—is a handful of grass worth dying for? There are other places—"

"I have been other places," Fiersen told her gently, "and the grass is only a part of it. I came back to this ranch to stay."

He could feel her will beat against his face. "You would rather die than give up Bar D?"

He came forward a little. Put big scarred hands on the edge of the wagon. Light touched his face from Ed Cantlicker's windows, revealing the taciturn unbending look of him. "Fiersens," he said, "have always

107

owned Bar D. So long as I'm living they'll continue to own it."

"What will you do?"

He rolled up a smoke, giving this chore a considerable care. But when it was made, he suddenly tossed it away. He said, "Wait here," and went up the worn steps into Cantlicker's store.

"Slank," Cherry said, speaking out of the silence, "can't you stop this thing?"

"The rustling? Far as I know Jade's not—"

"Of course he's not doing it! But he means to fight back—you just know he does!"

"If he does there's nothin' I could say that'll stop him."

"And if there was, you wouldn't say it—that's about the size of it, isn't it?"

"Would you have him run like a damn whipped dog?"

"I don't want him *dead!*" Cherry cried emphatically.

"It does your womanly virtues justice."

How like him, she thought, to take that tone with her. How like this man with his tied-down guns to deride what he knew was clean and decent. He had a strong and broad-featured face seen in the light from Cantlicker's. A handsome face and a half smiling negligence that hid his real thinking as those bland soft manners masked whatever was inside of him. A personable man, well turned out, more often taken for the rancher then Fiersen, who looked like thirty a month and found.

"I don't want him dead!" Cherry said again.

"I heard you. But ain't you being . . ." He let the rest go and buttoned his coat up.

Fiersen came down the steps and moved up to the wagon. Put several boxes of Winchester cartridges under the seat and, avoiding the girl's darkly frightened glance, nodded curtly at Calder.

"Let's go," he said. "You can handle the team can't you, Cherry? Lead off then. Slank and me will bring up the rear."

Cherry risked one last despairing question. "You're going to fight?"

Fiersen shrugged. "I don't figure to let them run me out of here."

ELEVEN

BUT WHEN THEY reached the laundry, over which the gambler had his quarters, she could not see in his present condition how

109

she'd get him up the dark rickety stairs that mounted the outside wall of the building. Frank purely could not make it on his own—it was out of the question.

Anyone could see how weak he was feeling; fine words couldn't hide it and, considering how much of his weight she was bolstering now, it seemed to her extremely doubtful that Frank could so much as stand, unaided.

She said dubiously, "Don't you think I had better . . ."

"Madam—" Endite drew himself up with a pitiful grimace. "I'm grateful to you. I really am. All my life, if God spares me, I'll treasure the memory. But you must go no farther—" He suddenly swayed, catching at the discolored wall for support, hanging there weak and shaking against it. Attempting to reassure her, with a terrible grimace, he pushed himself upright alone and unaided; but the weakened flesh finally failed him. Taisy knew he would have fallen if she hadn't grabbed onto him.

"I—I'll be all right," he mumbled. "I'll—I'll be quite myself . . . directly. You—you'd better go now, Miz Taisy."

"I won't be a-doin' no such thing!" Taisy cried. "The very idea!" It was plain she'd have to take a firm hand with him. He was in no shape to be left alone and, anyway, where could she go if she deserted him now? Not back to the Hairpin House—never there! That Lieutenant and Gooms were likely scouring the place for her; and if they weren't they would be. She said, quick and firm, "You're a-goin' to let me help you get up them stairs."

He stared and at last said irresolutely, "Well . . . just to the top, then."

"You'll be needin' a woman here," she declared, kind of breathless as they paused to conserve Frank's strength partway up. She eyed him nervously, knowing she had practically put the words in his mouth. But Frank didn't say them. He just kind of groaned and she felt purely glad it was dark enough here that Frank couldn't see the burning look of her cheeks. She felt mighty wicked. In a way she felt kind of sorry, too, taking advantage of him this way, and him so danged straight-laced and good. Kind of seemed like she hadn't ought to be doing this to him, him so highminded kindly, and such a terrible important fellow, too.

But she couldn't see any help for it. She was so fed up with Dry Bottom she could taste it. Almost anything, she thought, would be better than spending all the rest of her days getting pinched and grabbed and laughed at, waiting on that goldarn table. Probably wouldn't ever catch another chance like this to get shut of it. Educated fellows good-looking as Frank wasn't going to be thick as cloves around here. Someway she'd just got to make things happen so that, when Frank left, he would take her with him.

She guessed like enough this would take some doing, and felt herself to be terrible ignorant; but like her Paw had always said, there was more ways to skin a rabbit than one!—not that poor Frank was a dadburned rabbit. But unless he plain right-out said he didn't want her . . . Lordy! he wouldn't do that, would he? That would be too purely awful! Golly Moses! That would be the last straw!

She reckoned she had better be finding out pronto. No dang sense to be a ruined woman if . . . She said, "I'll hold onto you while you're a-gettin' your key." And, when he pushed open the door, "I'm a-goin' in with you, Mister Endite—I wouldn't dast to have you dependin' on yourself, in the dark and all, and you so weak as a wrung-out chicken. I aim to see you get fixed up proper."

Endite, through the contortion of pain he had put on his face, could scarcely credit such good luck as this, and had a momentary wonder if he'd been mistaken. After all, her mother . . . Could any girl actually be this by God ignorant? Too dark, of course, but he'd have liked right then to get a clear look at her.

He growled, "Proper young ladies don't go into men's rooms, not if they value their reputations. I cannot allow you—"

"You ain't got much choice; you're in mighty poor shape to be a-carin' for yourself. Why, I wouldn't dast trust you with a lamp right now—you're that weak you might drop it and set the place afire! Suppose you was to fall down—how'd you ever get up? Why, even with me here to steady you, it's all you can do to hold yourself up."

Endite bent his head so she wouldn't see him grin. She was about the easiest piece he had ever tied into; but he guessed he'd better warn her again, just to be on the safe side. Might go extremely hard with him if she'd to go away later and claim he'd lured her . . .

"Bless you," he said, "from the bottom

of my heart," and let his voice break on a note of pure anguish. He clung with both hands to a section of the door, his breath making a harsh, heavy panting. "But—but I cannot allow you to . . . to throw away your good name, ma'am. I'll manage some- way—"

She had no mind to be put off with such rubbish. "Where-at's the lamp?" she asked, brushing past him. "Where are the matches?"

Maybe, he thought, he should pass out at this point; but decided against it. Dry Bot- tom would never swallow such hogwash. Might induce folks to consider her in the light of a victim. This wasn't the kind of deal a man should get careless with.

He squeezed out a faint groan. "Lamp is . . . is on the sideboard—"

"I've found the matches," she said, and struck one.

The place smelled of stale cigar smoke. She threw open a window to let in more air. He watched her put the lighted lamp down and, disheveled though she was, he couldn't remember ever seeing a more pleasing pic- ture. The little hat set off her hair and the soft glow lent it a look of burnished copper. She pretty near took Frank's breath away.

It was the first time tonight he'd got a really clear look at her. He could not think where she had gotten the duds but they certainly smartened her, draping her lines and long legs to advantage.

Frank couldn't hardly take his eyes off her. He did manage, however, while she'd been busy with the lamp, to get the door shut and move a bit farther into the room.

She came over to help him. "Lordy, lordy!" she cried, suddenly aghast. "Why, your side's all over blood, Mister Endite! I've got to get you to bed and go fetch a doctor—"

Endite waved that aside. Last thing he wanted in this business was a doctor. And yet . . . He'd told her the truth, that he wasn't badly hurt; and what more could any sawbones say? And if after that she insisted on staying . . . Would it not be considerable in his favor to have old Crailvine hear her? To have him witness she had stayed up here of her own free will?

He took care to flounder rather badly as she helped him toward the bed. When she got him to it, he dropped upon it, gasping. He knew his complexion was always pale, and with that blood all over it would look even more so. He let pain have its way with him and, with legs hanging off the bed, he went limp.

Between nearly shut lids he watched a horrified expression pass over Taisy's features. She was scared, all right. "Lordy, lordy!" She tried to get his legs up. With them dangling there limp, it should be quite a task for her. He watched the changing shadows stretch across her throat and down the neckline of her dress as she bent over him. And his heart thumped faster as he considered, with lusty eagerness, the culmination of his intentions.

He lay with eyes closed once she'd got his legs up and straightened him. He heard her cross to the door, heard it open and close. But not until the sound of her feet left the stair did he open his eyes and grin up at the ceiling. This would be real sport! And, beside the hours he would spend teaching her things, there was the added attraction of being able, playing sick, to stay clear of that business being framed against Fiersen. That was one galoot he didn't want any truck with.

He'd thought, right at first, he might tip the man off, but had afterward decided against this. Remembrance of Tarlton's words was too strong. His health would be better if he remained strictly out of it, aside from that confrontation with Strawn.

He considered the girl's lush ripeness and chuckled.

She was not gone long and the doc came back with her; he could hear them coming up the outside stairs. He lay back as though plumb frazzled. Crailvine came querulously into the room, setting his bag on a chair by the bed. Endite was not going to try to fool Doc—not, that is, about his physical condition. When the man stood over the bed peering down at him, Endite said, "I've tried to tell her, Doc, that wasn't no—"

"I'll do the talking," Crailvine said. He did not have what is often described as a 'bedside manner.' "Looks like you've lost quite a passle of blood—never supposed a gambler could have had that much in him. Feelin' pretty puny, are you?"

"Hell, a little rest ought to rightly take care of it," Frank said, careful to strike the right note for this fellow. "Just a scratch, like I told her—"

"Scratch, is it?" Crailvine loosened Frank's clothing. "Get me a bucket of hot water, young lady. Now you listen to me," he told Endite. "The only thing certain about a gunshot wound is that the human animal fares better without one. All sorts of complications can set in—blood poisoning for one thing. Gangrene, for another. Lockjaw. More shot-up fellows die of lockjaw—"

"You're scarin' the lady, Doc. I'll be back dealing faro—"

"You'll be flat on your back for the next couple weeks!" Crailvine said with acerbity. "Don't tell me what you'll be doing!" He threw a look at the girl. "Better fetch some clean rags, too—and hurry it up, will you?"

Endite saw the frightened, bewildered look of her. "Have to get them from the laundry downstairs," he said. "Guess Charley'll have to heat up the water—does it *have* to be hot?"

"I don't think cold water would do you much good," the doctor snapped testily; and Taisy went banging off down the stairs. Over his glasses, Crailvine looked a long time at Frank. "That your sister?"

Endite considered alternatives, discarded them. "Stack Aiken's girl," he said and watched Crailvine's brows climb over the glasses. "Helped me up here and insisted she get you to come have a look at me. Been hashing at the hotel."

"So that's old Stack's kid . . . . I'd never

have guessed it. Don't seem to favor the Aikens much."

He took off his cheaters and polished them, thoughtfully tapped them against wrinkled cheek, but did not say anything; nor did Frank.

Taisy came presently back with some rags and the water. Doc, eyeing her curiously, went abruptly to work. When he put his tools away and straightened, he said, "Expect you'll live through it," and slanched a look at the girl again. She was still standing there by the foot of the bed, pale, kind of moon-eyed, watching Frank's face.

The man did look pretty well whipped out, but the bullet had not lodged in him. It hadn't cut anything important, nor broken or splintered any ribs. An ugly looking wound, but that was the size of it.

Crailvine took off his glasses and puffed on them, polished them with a handkerchief while his stare went over Taisy Aiken again. A well set-up little piece, he thought, and wondered how well she knew Frank Endite. None of his business, of course, but it was in his mind Frank had a pretty sharp way with the ladies.

Said Endite from the bed, "You can see her home, can't you?"

She chose that moment to say with devastating frankness, "I ain't a-goin' home. I ain't a-goin' to work at the hotel no more. I'm a-figurin' to stay right here and take care of you—"

"But my dear young lady! You don't understand," Frank protested. "I appreciate your concern, but . . . Dang it, you tell her, Doc!" and met Crailvine's interested stare with the look of a man who asks counsel and guidance, but the doctor did not offer any.

It was no part of Frank's notion to have Taisy leave, but this was treacherous ground and a man had to be careful what impression flew round. It wasn't an easy thing to manage; just the nearness of her made Frank's whole body tingle. He couldn't have Crailvine divining his intentions. He wanted Doc to be able to testify later Frank Endite was acting entirely in good faith.

She made an appealing figure in the lamp's yellow glow. Somewhat hoydenish yet forlornly lovely. She made Frank think of a captured lioness, spirit half broken by wounds and imprisonment yet ready in an instant to show its claws. She had that wildness about her, that untameable quality, that pulse-lifting strangeness in the way she looked at you. Then again, he thought, in her bedraggled frock, she was rather like some ungainly Magdalene, with that little hat gone awry on her curls and those rich copper locks so piquantly framing that scared little face. Such a child she seemed, although—like a bursting blossom—so alive with promise. He found it difficult to concentrate with those great dark eyes so wistfully regarding him.

He wished the damned doc would get himself out of here, yet realized he had to put a brake on his impatience. She had to be thought to remain in this place entirely against his wishes. He said, "Miz Taisy, ma'am—" and threw out a helpless hand toward Crailvine. "Can't you convince her, Doc?"

Crailvine pursed his wrinkled lips.

Taisy exclaimed with eyes wide and bright, "Why can't I stay with him? What's so . . . so *peculiar* about me a-carin' for him? He ain't got nothin' that's catchin' and anyone can see he ain't up to tendin' to himself. You said he'd have to stay in that bed—"

Endite growled with a pain-wracked breath, "Good lord! Have you no worry for what folks might think? About what might be said of an unmarried female setting up here with a gambler accused of cheating at cards?"

"But you didn't!" Taisy said, blushing furiously. "That brand inspector said you didn't . . . Anyway, I wouldn't be caring what folks thought. Don't you be a-worryin' about me. Why, I ain't hardly no more account in this town than a . . . than . . . than a dadburned horse apple!" She stood twisting a fold of her skirt in frustration. She had, someway, a dignity Endite hadn't recalled. It was astonishing how excited she looked. Made her eyes darker and deeper. The yellow glow edged lifted chin and rounded the shape of her firm young breasts, lay warm and mellow against the fullness of her throat. Frank shut his eyes lest they give him away.

He had never imagined she could be like this.

Even Doc looked affected by her.

Unaware, Taisy plunged on. "You know there won't nobody get lathered up over no horsethief's daughter. Don't be thinkin' no more about me—let me do any worryin' that's needed. I can bed on the sofa in that other room—I can be mighty handy, you'll see. I can cook. I can change his bandages. You tell him, Doc Crailvine."

Frank looked at the doctor. Crailvine smiled. He picked up his bag. "I reckon that's settled. Not a bad idea to have someone around."

"But a *girl!*" Endite growled.

"You know any men that would do as much for you? She won't be the first girl to nurse—"

"But the wag of tongues, man! In a burg this size—I'm an unmarried man and Taisy here—hell, she's just a kid!"

"Oh, there might be a little talk," Doc conceded.

"The female buzzards that roost around here—"

"If a girl makes up her mind to be a nurse, she's got to start someplace. Just because you happen to be her first patient—"

"Now you know damn well—"

"But the town won't, will it?" Crailvine peered at the girl. She must think quite a heap of Frank Endite; kind of made him think a mite better of Frank himself. Funny, he mused, the kind of galoots some women got their hearts set on, fellers that wouldn't fetch them nothing but troubles. Maybe she hoped to make a better man out of him. Women got them kind of notions.

Sighing, Doc picked up his hat and bag. "I'll look in on you tomorrow."

"Then I can stay?" Taisy asked.

Old Doc shrugged. "In your place I wouldn't, but if you're certain sure that's what you want, I don't see how Frank'll be able to stop you."

TWELVE

FIERSEN FOLLOWED THE rattle and bang of the wagon with thoughts much the color of the night about him. The storm had long since crawled off and gone, following the mineralized crags of the Ritas, crossing the Rincons to hammer and blast at the Catalinas with rain whipping at them like sand from a busted hourglass. But never so much as a drop where it was needed.

Fiersen shrugged off his mood and peered ahead at the wagon. Calder rode at his side and he, too, was silently considering the wagon where it rattled and bumped as it crept past the wavering fronds of grease-wood.

Fiersen grimaced. When a man started

124

thinking, he had left youth behind. In the old days, working around his father's ranch, he had thought this country bred a life of hardship, a life tough with work and damn little fun in it. Turned women old before their time. A life of heartbreaking drudgery he'd thought it—but that was before he'd gone off to Texas. Before he had ridden with Ketchum and watched that dead marshal fall through the smoke. Now, he believed, if he could go back to those days he would know content.

But you couldn't go back. There was no turning back for anyone.

This Santa Cruz country was still a good place with its quiet and blue distances; the kind of a land that could entice better visions than a man knew existed. This vast Arizona was clean windswept earth. Nothing puny about it. Called up all a man's strength to admire it, shaped to every mood and purpose. Embraced within its spacious bounds could be found just about every kind of climate; all sorts of animals; big game, too—lobos, coyotes, mountain lions and grizzlies; elk and antelope and mule-tailed deer; mountain sheep, javelinas, and birds driven out of more settled places. Great reaches of timber, grassy plains; and mountains from whose crests upon clear days you could see great dun stretches of desert, barren, sweltering, windswept and lonely, thirteen thousand feet below. Fiersen loved every tumbled rock and wind-scoured bastion, every mile of those blistering wastes, with a deep intense loyalty nothing could change. And, for him, the finest was right where he was, here in the Santa Cruz valley where the masked bobwhite whisked his cheery call.

He knew its possibilities, discerned how the valley and its hemming mountains could be built into a mighty cattle empire, a kingdom bigger than some eastern states. He knew someone else was absorbed in this vision. Someone who cared so little for his neighbors, he could brush them aside without compunction, deliberately pit them against one another, ruin, uncaringly cripple and kill them—and it had already started. Burr Rubelcaba had seen to that.

Rubelcaba and Fiersen were both big men; big owners, too, though Burr was the bigger now, hiring twice as many riders, spreading his herds wherever no owner would stand up against him. Both had tough crews; Fiersen because he would do what he could to protect his interests, living in an age of transition and violence. The East had been turning out Boss Tweeds and the West was creating Doolins and Daltons, with the law a plumb joke all across the country.

Fiersen believed in giving men a chance, another reason he'd been hiring men of dubious antecedents; drifters who seldom spoke, but all of whom had the same quickness of movement, the same hard scrinched-up stare.

Rubelcaba, Fiersen thought, had all the joviality and openhanded sentiment of a prime bully. He was one of those who believed that everything belonged to the man with the guts to take it and would never be satisfied with anything less than he was able to grab. He was what was coming to be called a cattle baron. No ordinary man could ever hope to achieve what Rubelcaba wanted in his lifetime, and he had what it called for, plus the kind of crew to whom fair play and scruples were nothing but terms to be laughed at. He'd come into this country ten years ago with a handful of broncs and a ragged bedroll. Few of his neighbors recalled that now, but Fiersen remembered; remembered the antagonism of that first meeting, the brag Rubelcaba had flung in his face.

He'd come with his broncs and his bed-roll and squatted on ten sections of the country's poorest range, land cut up by draws and gullies, windswept and eroded, good for nothing at that time but wolves and cactus. The man had seen it as a foot-hold, an unwanted crack in the valley's lush-ness. Rubelcaba had got his boot in that crack and nothing had ever dislodged him.

Fiersen remembered those days very well. He'd been just an overgrown kid at the time and had ridden out to look the newcomer over, to find out if he could what this stranger was like. And big Rubelcaba—he'd been big even then, had shown him. In his raggedy clothes and discolored old hat, the stranger had looked Fiersen over and laughed.

"I get it now," the stranger had sneered. "Your old man's the brass-collar dog in these parts," and had given that scornful bark of a laugh. "Reckon you come out here to lord it over me. Well, don't try it, sonny—I could shoot them buttons off your shirt with one eye shut! Go on, now—git goin'. Clear out! I got no time to waste foolin' with kids!"

"Don't you want any friends?" Fiersen had asked incredulously.

"Friends! What's them for? Can't eat 'em, can you? Can't put 'em in your pocket. Friends! You tryin' to make me laugh? This here's my friend!" and he'd slapped the big pistol that rode at his hip. "Take a good look at him so's you'll remember. Your old man better get a hump on himself before he gets bogged down and plumb choked on my dust!"

Then, suddenly, he'd scowled. "Don't believe me, eh? Guess you figure I'm shootin' my mouth off. Ten years from now I'll be ownin' this country—tell your old man that! Now get the hell outa here!"

That was Rubelcaba ten years ago.

It hadn't quite come true but he was working at it. Had upwards of two hundred thousand acres under wire—no one could guess how many cattle he had. His horse-flesh, founded on Shiloh blood by way of Whalebone and Billy, was the fastest stock in the land. Amazing what the man had accomplished in these short years. A real hustler. He had, folks said, the Midas touch. Certainly everything he tackled showed a quick prosperity. His steers were the biggest, his horses the fastest, and the men he employed the toughest in the country. Still, he kept losing cows—or claimed he did.

Fiersen didn't notice whereabouts in the journey Michael Strawn had got himself up off the wagon bed. Strawn was on the seat beside Cherry Grant when the wagon pulled into the Bar D yard. Fiersen wasn't thinking of Strawn at the moment but was recalling something Calder had said about man being born to trouble. Maybe there was a touch of the prophet in Calder. Certainly Fiersen had hoped to be done with trouble when he'd quit Ketchum five years ago and come back home to turn over a new leaf. Began to look now like he was a long ways from done with it.

He could hear Gyp, the dog, barking round the wagon, and Strawn telling the dog to shut up, and Cherry's tired tones mixed into Strawn's grumbling. Then Cherry said, "What is it to you?" with a quick flare of temper. "Let me alone!" And Strawn's voice, indescribably bitter; but did not try to make out the man's words. They were always quarreling, always hurting each other.

"Want I should take your horse?" Calder asked, pulling up.

"Cherry going home?"

She heard him and answered. "I'll spend

the night here—no use waking Jordie to go home this late."

Fiersen tiredly climbed out of the saddle. Calder wheeled away with his horse in tow.

Fiersen's mind still circled his problems. In a remote kind of way, he listened to the hoof falls receding corralwards and Strawn still grumbling as he unharnessed the team. "We can fetch these things in the morning," Cherry murmured, and the sound of her boots moved across the gallery.

Still Fiersen remained in the windy dark, thinking, looking wistfully up at the far shine of stars. And was still there, still probing his thoughts, when he heard Strawn slam the bunkhouse door. And for all this thinking, he felt no better. But his mind was made up to one thing. He might die in this country but he was damned if he'd be shoved out.

THIRTEEN

IN THE DEEPEST black just before dawn, a rider came quietly into the trees of the shallow depression known as Cottonwood Seep on the southeast edge of the Spanish Cross holdings. There he pulled up and softly whistled twice. An answering whistle came out of the dark and a dismounted man cuffed his chaps and got up. "Thought mebbe you wasn't comin'," he said.

"Made it soon as I could," the rider answered. "If you know anybody will suit you better, you've my leave to get 'em—I ain't stuck on this clambake."

He made a formless unguessable shape in this gloom and the man who had waited kept out of sight. He said with a grunt of a laugh, "You'll do first rate till some ranny catches you. What'd you find out? How's he figure this deal? Suspicious, is he?"

"Ain't made no remarks, but in town this last trip he bought a heap of cartridges. Never said two words all the way home. I been told it might pay us to look into what he was doin' that time he was away five-six years ago."

" 'Fore his old man croaked, you mean?"

"What I was given to understand. Look at it this way. Here's a kid raised up by an ol' catawampus that's had to sweat plenty for everything he got. From what I hear his kid got the same. They say Jade never got a nickel for his work; an' no mother around to soften the bumps for him. No chance to blow off, just work an' more of it. Twenty-two years is a powerful long time to be buildin' up steam. What would you do, gettin' loose of that?"

"We ain't talkin' about me. My ol' man," said the fellow who had waited, "was a bar-room drunk—don't ask me what no Fiersen would do. I'm payin' you to find out these things."

"All right; keep your shirt on. Your money ain't payin' to find out what he *done*. I got all I can handle keepin' track of what he's doin'."

The rider hoisted his shoulders and hunched himself forward. "You ever tried scratchin' your ear with your elbow? That's a plumb easy chore beside the one you give me. And ears don't pack no guns on 'em, either."

The man in the shadows let the silence build up, saying finally, unfavorably, "There's damn little room for cold feet on my payroll."

The galoot on the horse hauled his back up stiffly. "Listen, Rubelcaba. I've worked like hell for what you been payin'. Anytime I don't suit just jump off an' say so."

"Any time you don't suit me, you'll know it. So long's we see eye to eye you're in clover. When we don't you won't be around no more."

He stood there a moment, then said more agreeably, "Vance ain't likin' the way things are goin'—got a burr up his ass. He's howlin' for action. Whereabouts is the most of Fiersen's cows bedded down?"

"My God!" exclaimed the rider. "You don't figure Vance aims to run off some of Fiersen's. Why, Jade would just about bust a gut."

"Mebbe that's what Vance wants," Rubelcaba murmured. "You're gonna wear that brain of yours out one of these days. Now you take me. When a chance for big winning lopes my way, I don't argue about it. Be a good policy for you to practice."

He got out his Durham, shook his head and put it back. The expression on his face wasn't visible in this gloom but irritation rasped in his voice. "Try answerin' my question."

"Huerfano Butte," said the rider reluctantly. "But I tell you, Ru—"

"Never mind—never mind. Heard you the first time. You got any notion what's to be found on Jade's backtrail?"

"I don't even know where he was but from what I hear tell he come back here five years ago. How long has it been since they hanged Jack Ketchum?"

134

Vance, riding for home at the head of his crew, said, "This country's changin' pretty damn fast."

Teke, the Turkey Track range boss, lifted his cowman's face and nodded.

"I don't like it," Vance growled.

Teke didn't feel this called for comment.

"Used to be," Vance grumbled, "this was damn fine country. Ol' Man Fiersen was running things then. You could pick out your friends; didn't have to watch every word you turned loose of. Wasn't much rustlin' and mighty few strangers. Now these hills fairly crawl with drifters. Used to be when you looked at a man you knew him; now I'll be damned if you know who you know."

"Yeah. It's this Texas riffraff you got to watch out for."

"Is it?" Vance said. "Sometimes I wonder!"

"Just look at the faces," Teke pointed out. "Take any ten men you kin clap your eyes on. Six of 'em every time's goin' to be strangers, an' four of them anyway is goin' to be gunfighters. Country's fillin' up."

"I don't like it," Vance muttered. "I don't like change. Sometimes, ridin' round, I get to thinkin' about things an' you know, by God, it frightens me!" He stared at the starlit trail, darkly scowling; thus missed entirely the look Teke slanched him. Which, Teke might have told you, was what come from thinking. A man could be trapped in such webs of absorption; it could take your mind straight away from things you could ill afford not to notice. Vance said, "I used to allow I knew my neighbors; I can't tell anymore if they're friends or not."

"Storm's swingin' round," Teke observed.

His boss sent a badgered look at the clouds. "Ain't it never going to rain around here no more?" He let go of a snort that rasped with outrage. "Even the goddam climate's changin'!"

"Nature's way," Teke said. "Did you know Buck Yates sold off that foothills range? I got it pretty straight that he's sold himself plumb out of the hills."

Vance's head came up like a rope had jerked it, swinging a startled edgy look at his foreman. The light was too dim for him to catch the man's expression. "Yates promised to give me first chance on that!"

"Well, he's sold it," Teke said again. "Blakely's sold, too. Reckon you can see that puts us right up against Fiersen's fence—"

"Fiersen's!"

"Yeah," Teke grinned in the dark. "Fiersen bought them both out I been told. If he wants your grass he'll likely get that, too."

Vance exploded. When he'd reeled in his voice to hog-calling pitch again, the foreman said in a dry tone of censure, "You can see now where that ruckus of yours leaves us. I wouldn't be surprised if he dug up the hatchet."

"But what would Fiersen want with that range?"

"Ain't you noticed he's got growin' pains? Hell, I thought you knew no Fiersen could be satisfied with what he's got. Aims to see that Bar D iron of his—"

"No. You've got him wrong," Vance said, shaking his head; and he stared at Teke disbelieving, incredulous. "He ain't like that. A little toplofty, mebbe a little inclined to have his own way, but he would have to be plumb wild—"

"Wild!" Teke snorted. "Looks to me like he's wild to control this whole country. He'll do it, too, if folks don't get a wiggle on. This cow stealin's part an' parcel of it. Go

after these outlyin' outfits first—run off their
cattle, shoot'em up, scare'em. When a man's
got his whole pile sunk in a place, it ain't
goin' to take much to get his wind up.
When he sees plain ruin starin' down his
gullet, he'll snatch for the first cash price
he's offered. Then good old Jade buys him
out, plumb legal."

He let the quiet close round them while
Vance digested this. "Trouble with you,"
he presently remarked, "is you don't want
to believe what your own eyes tell you. You
keep thinkin' that cow thief's your friend,
like he used to be. Common horse sense
should tell you he's the galoot back of
whatever's goin' on around here. Let me tell
you somethin', Mister Vance. When a man
starts buildin' up a spread like his, friendship's just a friggin' word to him. I tell you
that feller's out to swaller this valley!"

"You don't believe that, surely—"

"Ain't a case of believin'. All you've got
to do is add it up. Look around. That
galoot's gone bronc! While you been makin'
excuses for him, he's layin' pipe to clean
you out. That bonehead play you pulled
tonight will cost you more'n you can ever
git back; nobody'll put any stock in your
judgment. You had that bunch worked up

for a showdown and let that sidewinder wangle you out of it. You let a lot of boys down that figured you meant business. You didn't see Rubelcaba stickin' *his* jaw out. There's the gent folks'll look to now."

Teke could feel his words eating into Vance. He knew which things would gouge Vance the deepest and unsparingly used them. Vance, though having a good deal of bottom, also had his share of blind spots. Man's injustice to man upset him. He had a kind of leaning, it seemed like, for persons other people had got pretty much fed up with. He wanted to believe the world a better place than his own experience indicated. His liking for people made him see too many sides of a thing for him ever to take decisive action. Tonight's confrontation with Fiersen was something he'd been maneuvered into and he couldn't right now imagine why he'd braced Jade.

Vance liked to be well thought of, liked to feel on terms of trust with folks around him; liked to think they put considerable weight in his notions; these were the things Teke's talk had clawed at, the foundation stones of the man's vanity.

Now, having put Vance's mind in an uproar, Teke shifted the talk to pleasanter pastures. "That brat of Stack Aikens' is gettin' plumb developed—you notice her tonight? Wonder what she sees in that two-by-four card sharp? Wonder where she got them duds she was wearin'—"

"You sure them fellers sold out to Jade?"

"Yates an' Blakely? Alls I know is what Yates told me. Him an' his missus was pilin' their belongin's into a wagon. Goin' to Alamagordo—said they'd bought a little property west of town. Kinda sounded like it might be out in that White Sands desert."

"Fiersen," Vance said, "ain't got no fence. You know he never believed in—"

"What I been tryin' to tell you, ain't it? Yates' place is fenced; Blakely's too. They both border us, bein' between us an' Fiersen. It's them's been keepin' Bar D critters from gettin' all over our Turkey Track range. How long you figure he'll leave up them fences? How long can you last if he pulls 'em down? You better git up and git a move on. That jasper means business."

"All right—all right," Vance said. He scowled around like a badgered catawampus.

"Looks to me," Teke prodded, "like we're on the toboggan. You got to fight fire with fire in this world. You can't put it out with no chaw of tobacker!"

"If the fence is down—"

"If the fence is down, you might's well emigrate."

"We could put up another."

Teke's acid voice said, plainly disgusted, "We ain't got the time to put up a new fence. We ain't got the men an' we ain't got the money. Even if we had, what good would it do? How kin we watch ten miles of wire?" He looked at Vance with some suggestion of scorn. "If that fence is down, we got just one chance."

He could sense Vance's stare, even feel Vance's thoughts running round like a bird dog snuffling at a whiff of lion. "Do I have to make you a picture of it?"

That much he said and shut his mouth, knowing the way Vance's mind would pick at it. "Maybe," Vance said, irascibly uncertain, "maybe you better."

"All right. Only way you kin stop Fiersen from throwin' his steers all over your grass is to hit him first—and I mean right now."

"How?"

"You ain't gonna like it."

"How?" Vance repeated.

"By throwin' your beef onto Fiersen's grass. And for good measure, mebbe you could sling a little lead in his direction."

"You think he'll stand still—"

"Won't have much choice if you work it right. Thing to do is keep him hustlin' an' dodgin'—never let him dig in. Throw down on his crew ever' time they're in gunsight." Teke took a deep breath, saying sharply: "When a man turns wolf, he don't recognize friends; you better remember it. Fiersen's out t' git his any way that he's able. You got to do likewise if you aim to stay healthy."

Vance rode quite a distance without comment, without any sign of the struggle he was making. This was the blackest hour, just before dawn, the time when a man's gumption reached its lowest level. No man of the crew behind them spoke. Some of them probably, more than half horse, were dozing in the saddle. Wasn't much sound but the hoof falls of their ponies, the groan and skreak of leather, jingle of curb chain and rowel. The dark was wrapped like a blanket about them, like the pulled-up folds of a highwayman's kerchief.

Vance said out of that black quiet abruptly, "Reckon we better have a look at that fence. If the wire is down . . ." He let the rest of it go and cut his horse on a tangent that would take them past the two sold spreads.

Teke, smiling in the gloom, led the crew after him. The nearest fence was not above a couple miles off where it climbed through the hills along the Bar D boundary. Day would soon catch them up and already Teke could hear an early cowbird chirping from a greasewood clump. At this increased pace, they should come onto the fence at about first light.

They rode steadily without talk and came against the fence with the first crags coming grayly out of the night. On Bar D range, they followed the wire and came in due course to where the five strands had been cut and carted off. Not a single fencepost showed beyond.

"Well," Teke said, morosely eyeing Vance. "I reckon this is it. You want to go after him now or—"

"We will wait," Vance said, "till we see what he's done where it borders us. If he's bought Yates out, he has a perfect right to tear out this part."

Teke found nothing on Vance's face that pleased him. Yet he kept his voice civil. "If he cut this end he's likely yanked the rest.

Time to strike is right now before he gets set an' ready for us."

"Nevertheless, we will look at the other end first."

Vance, wheeling his mount, put it through the gap and Teke with the crew went loping after him, strung out through the blue-gray light that picked out shapes thirty feet away and left all else a neutral blur that had no beginning nor observable end. They held to this larruping pace several minutes, forging purposefully into half-light ahead, with the murk closing in thirty feet behind and dogging them like a stalking lynx.

Far away in the gloom, a coyote yammered from some distant ridge; and Teke heard something more, which he'd listened for, but did not make any mention of this. Then of a sudden, Cliff Vance also heard; Teke knew when this was by the way his boss stiffened up in the saddle. Wondering if perhaps this might not be the best time, Teke dropped a hand beside his pistol, but Vance came alive too sudden for him.

"Cattle!" Vance yelled, and dragged up his rifle, slamming his horse so hard to the right that Teke, on his left, had no opportunity to complete his play.

"They're comin' dead at us!" a man back

of him cried; and pale shafts of light stabbed the gloom ahead, and out of the gloom of a dust-filled hollow came wild-eyed steers in a thundering sea of pounding hooves. Guns were popping like paper sacks, and almost before Teke knew what was happening, his horse swapped ends under him and went plunging over the ground they'd just covered with every ounce of energy in it. It was all he could do to keep his seat and the outstretched horns of those bellowing cattle seemed to him to be but a half jump behind.

Through the billowing dust, Vance caught fleeting glimpses of the harrying riders who were driving this herd, but never a chance in that lemon haze even to guess at these waddies' identity; only by the guessed direction of their travel could he imagine they were some of Jade's bunch. Several times he jerked up his rifle and winged off a shot but could not be certain if any of these connected. He was too much occupied with his terrified horse to effectively do more than grit his teeth at the dust-shrouded shapes veering round him. He saw one horse go heels over head and heard the high shriek of its agonized cry but could not see if there'd been a man in the saddle. A carbine abruptly spat blue flame at him and, somewhere behind, he heard the *thwunk* of its bullet and one man's shout sailed up and died.

One of his punchers burst out of the murk, swung a jittery horse in beside Vance and stared goggle-eyed at the steers pitching past them, firing his pistol until it was emptied.

Vance slammed the spent rifle into its boot, grabbed out his own belt gun, the pencil-thin flare from its barrel slashing into the pall with no more effect than a thrown match would make. Then, raking his pony's flanks with his spurs, the rest of the Turkey Track crew barreling after him, tore into the raucous clouds swirling round them, cutting round the near edge of the thinned-out cattle.

Lead laced the gloom with its tight-wire whining and out of that fog, Vance heard someone curse him; and he threw up his six-shooter and kept triggering futilely before recollecting he had not reloaded. A rocketing rider crashed headlong into him, horse striking horse with a staggering impact. Vance's mount lurched aside and went squealing back on its haunches, forefeet savagely flailing the air; Vance was so occupied fighting him down, he did not see what became of the other.

The fight was over; he realized that. Those rannies with the herd had gone tearing off through breaking brush, and with them went the last of his hopes for the future. The shock of this knowledge poured numbingly through him; the end of all years he had put into Turkey Track. Those gone-away riders with their bellowing stampeded beef told him plainer than words what he'd find at the ranch. This was the end and it sickened him.

He could hear his crew calling through the brush, shouting out their finds and their querulous questions; but these harsh cries had no meaning for him, no power to pull him out of his misery. The finish he envisioned was too entire for the thinking part of his mind to assimilate. He tried to rally himself, tried to build up a smoke, but shaking fingers kept tearing the papers. Through settling tatters of dust, he could hear the mumble of his crew's profane talk and presently, in the brightening light, these men drifted up and sat around him, silent and glowering. One man was afoot, and this fellow said with smoldering fury, "They got Tom Creig, the dirty sons!" And the fading sound of the disappeared cattle got thinner and thinner. Vance huddled in his saddle like an old, old man. And a long time later, Teke rode up on a limping pony whose glasseyed head hung limply down, when he stopped, between braced quivering legs.

Teke sat a while watching them, then brought his bleak stare up to probe Vance's face. "I been lookin'," he said, "at some of them cattle; every critter we dropped is packin' our brand. What do you say to that, Mister Vance?"

Vance let out a shuddery sigh. "Never mind," he said. "Take the boys on home."

"Take them home! Take them home, did you say?"

Vance wearily nodded, not bothering to look at him.

"And what are *you* fixin' to do, Mister Vance?"

"Turn wolf." Vance's voice was indescribably bitter.

Long will that night be recalled by those who lived through it in the Santa Cruz Valley, that night of August 30 when Mike Strawn shot Frank Endite in Dry Bottom's Sparrowhawk Bar. In that time and place, life was a thing geared to swift reprisal and

148

gunplay the invariable result and inevitable end of almost everything. Yet what an insignificant trifle to have powered such a string of horrendous events. Seemed as though Strawn's act were the cue for which all the inherent violence of the land had waited, spark to the powder, pin to the primer, flag to the straining horse. How the gods must have laughed that a man weak as Strawn could have loosed such a holocaust of doom on the country.

Summer's wind was soft in the grasses. Six-foot corn waved its yellowing tassels. Thousands of cattle, fat and careless, bedded in those basin ranges. In the south where the storm had earlier been, frogs were croaking in the rain-soaked open. Insects thrummed above greasewood flats and nighthawks swooped through the milo maize. On a distant ridge, a coyote yammered and rabbits browsed in the ranchwives' gardens. A land of plenty, a night of promise, abruptly raped by the crash of a pistol.

Where were men's minds that they could let this happen? Were they helpless sheep to be pushed and shoved at the herder's whim? Really men or chattering gophers?

Scarcely two hours after Endite's shooting, Death and Destruction took to the saddle. Greed tramped the valley with a twirling rope and Lust, like some jungle beast broken out of its cage, ran hog wild through the moonless night.

Far down the valley, south and east of Silva, twenty families of homesteaders were driven from their land at gunpoint, choused from their beds and herded like cattle toward a dirt road heading east, which they took. West of Dick's Peak, two small-spread ranchers were killed on their doorsteps.

A few miles beyond Tubac, six masked riders on stolen horses rode into Glaytem's ranchyard, tied up Ed and his womenfolks and leisurely proceeded to wreck the place; cut up his saddles and harness, knocked great holes in the walls of his home, smashed the roofboards into kindling, broke up furniture, gutted every horse in his pens and stable. Setting fire to his haystacks, they rode away.

Nearer Dry Bottom, yet still at some distance, between the towns of Carew and Proctor, the Mailstell family was visited also. Masked horsemen dragged all the furnishings out of the house, all gear and tools from the outbuildings, piled this collection against the rear wall of the barn and fired it.

At Amado, three masked men rode up to the home of Chico Valdez. They roped Valdez and his wife to the bedposts and disported themselves with the Valdez daughter, a Madonna-faced girl just turned fourteen.

At Mesquite, three women were shot in cold blood.

Near Continental, just before dawn, seven masked men astride Bar D horses swept up to the ranch of Elihu Baker, dragged him out of his bed and hanged him, shooting two cowboys who attempted to interfere. They poured kerosene into the feed bins and departed, leaving the place in flames.

At Twin Buttes, crippled old Thuston Blaggs was dragged from his house and drowned in his cesspool.

Vance's foreman, Teke, with his disgruntled crew, rode up to the smoldering remains of the home place; not a thing of value had escaped the fire. Nothing left of the log buildings but ashes. Vance's blooded stallion lay hamstrung in the dooryard. Most of the broodmare band had been slaughtered. The crew stood around pale of face, grimly silent. It was Teke who did the swearing for them. He called Jade Fiersen every name he could think of. The Turkey Track hands began oiling their guns.

Vance, after the others had left him, wandered aimlessly about, miserably checking the slaughtered mares; couldn't seem to collect his thoughts; could only stand gloomily sagged against the sharp edge of the dreams he had cherished. The sun coming out of the rose-banded east found him still there, like he walked in his sleep, waiting for someone to wake him.

He thought he needed a drink; thought perhaps a smoke might help, but continued to stand around staring and seeing over and over the work and the years he'd put into this place; it was like something had been torn out of him. He wasn't the man he had been five hours ago.

He kept smelling the dust, hearing the rumble and thunder of hoofs, the shouting, the curses, the crack-crack of rifles—kept living it over, and always behind each and every other thing was that abiding, paralyzing sense of disaster. It was a towering wave rushing over his head.

Gradually the tumult inside him subsided, the roaring went out of his aching head. He began to tremble and that, too, passed; he felt cold and numb; then his mind began working.

He realized he was finished in this country; he knew Jade Fiersen for a thorough man. Whatever Jade put his hand to, you could rest assured there'd be no half measures. Nothing tangible would be left of Turkey Track.

But why had he done this?

He couldn't believe that fight last night in the Sparrowhawk could have set Fiersen onto him. He'd never held with Jade's tumultuous ways, but they had grown up together, been friends for years, sharing experiences, time after time sharing even the same blanket. They'd had the same taste in horseflesh. Never before last night had they fought and he tried to think how that had come about but couldn't remember.

Jade.

Odd how well that name seemed to fit the man. No one had called him that in the old days; but he wasn't that free and easy kind anymore. He'd been named Jordan Fiersen and, mostly, what folks had called him was Jord. Jade. Something hard, smooth and polished. There was damn little polish about him but the rest of it fit well enough. Hard as stone since he'd come back from his wanderings. Fists like sledges. Some thought the name was for the color of his eyes, but Vance suspected it had sprung from the eye for an eye reactions of the man. Those who tampered with him could hardly expect him to turn the other cheek.

Vance would have laughed had anyone said such a thing in the old days. The man who came back to this range from wherever he'd been was a whole lot different from the one who went away. In those faraway places, something had considerably changed him. He seldom smiled these days, and back of that flint-like stare was something indomitably bleak; you could feel his will like the shove of a hand—you could almost feel he didn't want your friendship. This was one of the reasons Vance had stayed away from him; he was too hair-triggered.

Take the case of Juke Krantz.

Krantz had been a small-spread rancher, a shiftless person with an irritating habit of mavericking beef. Any unbranded animal of unknown ancestry was considered a 'maverick' and there'd been a time, not long ago, when such was considered the legitimate property of the first man to put his iron on it. But abuse had made the practice heavily frowned upon; too many mavericks had been manufactured.

Some gents who were short on morals and long on rope had found too quick ways of building a herd. They'd see a nice little calf tagging along after mama and, if mama packed a brand, it was just too bad for her. A lot of things could happen; if none of these proved expedient, she'd likely find herself slaughtered. The brand would be skun out of her carcass and a new, unrelated mark put on the calf. Sometimes mama would not be molested but painful things would be done to baby's feet. Plenty of upright ranchers used to brand mavericks; but when cowboys saw this as a chance to set up a spread of their own, the practice was discontinued and anyone caught at it might find himself at the end of hemp.

Krantz kept right on building his herd, but since he never hit any ranch hard or too often, no one had been riled to the point of going after him. Fiersen proved to be the exception. He bumped into Krantz in Dry Bottom one evening. With characteristic bluntness, Jade said, "What have you done with those Bar D calves you appropriated?"

"I never took your calves!" Krantz blustered.

"You sure won't take any more," Fiersen said. "You light a shuck out of this country pronto."

Krantz went for his gun and that was the end of him.

Cold, hard and sudden—that was Fiersen.

No one had ever cared a rap about Krantz until Fiersen killed him. After that, you'd have thought he was the town's first citizen. They began dubbing Fiersen "that goddam gunslinger" and some less polite things you didn't say in front of ladies.

Vance scowled, shook his head and the scowl became, if possible, even more bleak. He reckoned he was still trying to find excuses for Fiersen. Teke was probably right; no one but a plumb fool would try to alibi Jade after what Vance had seen with his own eyes this morning. No matter what Fiersen had once been in this country, he was now, self proven, an out-and-out range roughing rustler. Of course he was! The man was gone bronc just as Teke and the rest of them claimed. Ambition, greed, the shoddy craving for size had warped and twisted all the good things out of him. Anyone who'd do what Jade had deserved nothing better than a rope around his neck—and that quickly!

And he would damn sure get one. This range had taken all it aimed to off him! Thinking back on it now, Vance allowed the Valley had come at the truth of it when they said Jade Fiersen had framed Juke Krantz. Maybe Krantz had spied Jade on one of these cattle grabbing excursions; or maybe he'd come onto evidence that would have convicted Jade of some other, as yet unguessed, crime.

"I've been blind," Vance thought, "a stupid fool!"

And he remembered how, one after another, Fiersen had rid himself of his father's ranch hands, replacing them with new men out of nowhere, bleach-eyed rannies no upright rancher would dream of paying out good money to. Only Mike Strawn, who'd been born on the place, had Fiersen held over from the former crew.

Easy enough to see why Jade had kept *him*. Strawn was cut from the same type of clay as the rest of that bunch. Plainly Fiersen had been intent on building a wild bunch of gun-hungry trigger-slammers with the idea of taking over this country.

Some way these notions made Vance shudder, but he could not doubt the truth of them. Little things, events which at the time had seemed to hold little significance, now tramped his mind in terrible magnitude. "Lord," he muttered, "why couldn't I have foreseen this before he ruined me?"

And he thought of Cherry Grant and the girl's unwed mating, of the fatherless kid she called Jordie; and gnashed his teeth that he could have been such an ass. He recollected something else in that moment. That until the return of Jade Fiersen five years ago, Mike Strawn had been known as the life of any frolic, a laughing waddy who no longer even smiled. Now, thinking back on it, it seemed Strawn's laughter had died on that night four years ago when Fiersen had rushed Doc Crailvine out there to fetch Cherry's baby into the world.

Why, they hadn't even known she was pregnant!

Other things crossed Vance's mind and, with a muttered curse, he wheeled his mount and set off for Bar D. Black hate rode with him and guided the reins; hate reddening the rowels of his silver spurs.

FOURTEEN

FRANK ENDITE LAY with eyes half closed and watched the girl as she moved about, making little tasks for herself to do that she might put off the confrontation she felt hovering over her. Both of them knew what issues were involved; leastways Frank presumed they did. He knew, certainly, and she had ought to. A woman grown, she must know something of life's little ways. If she did not know, she must have suspected to be frittering around as she'd been this past hour, never actually meeting his stare. A skittish filly. Just the way Frank liked them.

Well, nobody could say he hadn't given her fair warning. All the way from the Sparrowhawk. Hell, she couldn't be *that* dumb! Bound to know what he wanted. Naturally it excited her; he'd been excited, too, that first time—he hardly remembered the woman but his mind shied away from her; God knew how many others she'd had.

But Taisy . . . Hell, she was *different!* This would be her first time probably. Frank toyed with that thought and felt a smug satisfaction. He decided he liked most everything about her. He had never known anyone quite so impressionable, never had a girl to hang upon his words as she did.

He guessed he'd ought to say something; she'd soon be running out of things to do and he hadn't much doubt this silence was bothering her. He wondered how he ever had imagined she wasn't much for looks. These clothes spruced her up to where, despite everything, he found her downright handsome. He wondered where they had come from but, mostly, he wondered how she'd look in bed.

He grinned to himself. He'd got to curb this impatience. The girl was unsure of herself. It would be plumb foolish to scare her away before he was up to handling her. She was still just a filly, quick to startle, easy to alarm. Better to go slow and build up to it. She'd come round once she got used to him; this whole business of life, he reminded himself, was new to her; strange and, like enough, scary. He'd plenty of time. She'd come of free will and wouldn't run out unless she became frightened.

Anyway, she thought him bad hurt, suffering from shock and loss of blood. Good thing to remember. Doc had given him two weeks in bed, and that was where he proposed to stay until this country had rid itself of Fiersen.

Thought of the man made him glance toward his vest where Taisy had hung it over a chair back; and he grinned again, somewhat sly and sadistic. "Do you read?" he asked, glancing up to find Taisy looking over his few books.

She turned, and once more he discovered the astonishing magnetism of her. It stirred him like exotic music. "A little," she smiled, tipping a look at him wistfully. "I only just about can," she blurted; "I'm terrible ignorant. Ain't never had much chance for schoolin'—ain't read over three whole books in my life!"

"Did you enjoy them?"

"Well . . . I liked one of them pretty well."

"You may read some of mine if you'd like to."

"Oh, I would—I purely would, Mister Endite."

She looked pathetically pleased, he thought, frowning; and saw how quick her face was to change, how sensitive to each variation of feeling. He poked up a smile, astonished to see how quick she returned it with her eyes lit up, lips half parted like some delicate blossom about to unfold. He saw the enhanced rise and fall of her breathing.

A queer one, all right. But he loved the way those smiles lit her up—the whole shyly eager look of her. It was plain she'd had little if any experience. She would have few standards, few comparisons to guide her. He thrilled to the thought of being her teacher. What a strange, extraordinary person she was. To explore her mind might prove almost as exciting as the exploration he was figuring to launch. Strange discoveries might reward such a search, and the prospect of cultivating these wild fruits was one to fill him with a lift of anticipation. It was stimulation simply to look at her.

He gave a soft chuckle and saw how responsive she was to the mood of him. She said in that wistful mission-bell voice, "What are you findin' so funny, Mister Endite?"

He waved a languid hand. "I been thinking," he said, "of some of the things we might do when I'm better, the great times we'll have, the new places we'll go to," and gave her a smile, half amused, half tender. "Where have you been all my life, Taisy Aiken?"

He loved the way she blushed, her confusion, the way her eyes grew large, then shyly hid behind her lashes. The way they afterward peeped out at him, incredulous, excited. "I'm so all-fired ignorant," she declared, "so ignorant an' ugly I . . . I just never thought you'd be a-carin'."

"Lord, you're not ugly! You're the handsomest thing ever happened to me—you *are;* I mean it! Inexperienced maybe, but ignorant—never! Once we start going places, and I don't mean little burgs like Dry Bottom—*real* places—*big* ones . . . towns like *Tucson, Dallas, Santa Fe, El Paso!*" He began to chuckle again at the look of her.

Taisy, naturally, misconstrued his mirth. Embarrassment flooded her face with color; her dark eyes filled with humiliation. "You ain't meanin' that, Mister Endite? It ain't right in you to be a-makin' fun of me—"

"Fun of you! Why, bless you, ma'am, I'm entirely serious. I mean every word of it. Here—come sit beside me . . . let me hold your hand. There, that's better. Let's see you smile. Let me wipe away those tears—"

But Taisy, pulling back, stood up again. "I—I'll be a-goin' now, Mister Endite."

"Go!" the gambler cried. "What for?" Concern stared out of his widened eyes; real worry edged the tone of him. He got an elbow under him and, groaning, came half upright. "You can't mean that, ma'am! Whatever have I said to offend you? Whatever, I apologize. I wouldn't have you hate—"

"Hate you?" Those dark eyes looked at him strangely. "Lordy, Mister Endite!' Course I ain't a-hatin' you. It's—it's just that—that . . ." But she couldn't find the words to explain the state of emotions she herself couldn't rightly get a handle on. Her widened eyes filled again with tears which she struggled to contain as Frank, in alarm, got up off the bed. He took her cold little hands in his and, when she raised her piteous face, kissed her tenderly. With his big white handkerchief, he wiped away the trembling tears and led her to the bed again. Abruptly remembering he was next to death's door, he sank down heavily onto its edge and a groan slipped faintly through his grimacing lips.

At once she was all contrition, almost overcome with compassion for him.

He gradually waved her concern aside. "It's nothing," he assured, smiling wryly. "This foolish wound has sapped my strength. I'll be all right in a moment. I'll just sit a bit and catch my breath."

"But surely you ought to git in bed. The doctor—"

"How can I be resigned to bed when you talk of—surely, Taisy, ma'am, you aren't going to leave me in such a fix? Leave me when I've only just found you?"

He dragged up an arm that someway got itself closed around her. Then he pulled her to him, burying his face against her breast. "Taisy! Taisy! Don't ever leave me—I don't believe I could bear for you to go." He lifted imploring eyes and perhaps, at last, he was entirely sincere; it was his glance that now showed the shine of tears. "Say you'll stay," he pleaded. "I need you, Taisy— don't you understand that?"

Looking at him, she seemed strangely shaken, dark eyes growing round with wonder.

Raising his haggard face, he pulled her against him one more time. "Stay with me, Taisy," he cried at her hoarsely, arms tightening their hold while the fresh clean woman smell of her rushed all through him like some heady wine. "Let me teach you what life holds for those who are willing to stand up to it, face it squarely. For those stout of courage to follow their hearts. Let me open the box of life's treasures for you and count them out for you one by one. I could teach you things—could show you miracles you've never dreamed of. Oh, Taisy, Taisy! There is so much to living you've never known . . . love, music, romance, books . . . every treasure of the mind can be yours, all the beauties of the universe. Gold and silks and satins and silver! Perfumes from far-away places. Clothes and fine foods, fragrant wines and precious liqueurs—a thousand kinds of excitements and pleasures! There's nothing we couldn't do . . . no heights we could not scale *together*. If only you'd say you might learn to feel what I feel for you—say there's a chance!"

He was like a child crying out for the moon. Taisy's hand came up and smoothed his curls. Enchantment shone in her soft dark eyes. They seemed filled with a quiet transcendent glory. She caught his impassioned face in her hands and, with an inarticulate cry, bent her sweet young lips to his.

"Lordy, Mister Endite—I never thought you'd be *a-wantin'* me!"

FIFTEEN

FIERSEN LAY ON his bunk at the Bar D ranch, interminably twisting and turning until finally, with a groan of exasperation, he swung his feet to the floor and shoved himself up. Sore and stiff in every sinew, bone weary as he never had been, he still could not sleep nor quiet his churning thoughts, unable to drive off those doubts and apprehensions which endlessly tramped between himself and slumber.

He wheeled at a sound from the door behind him. In its opening, a white shape showed still as death itself. The room was dark but Fiersen guessed who stood there. Bare feet made no sound on the floor as she flowed toward him. She touched his arm and dropped her hand, standing there a long time watching him. Her voice was low, enwrapped in tension. "Is it that bad, Jord?"

"I expect it's going to be."

"What's back of it?"

"Greed, I reckon."

She peered at him queerly with her head

at one side. "I'm grown," she said. "You can tell me."

"Not much to tell. Somebody's after this valley—all of it."

She stared through a longdrawn stillness. Shivered a little. He put a hand on her arm. "Hang onto yourself," he said gently.

"Is it Vance? Is Cliff Vance the one?"

"I don't think so." He could see the bare shine of her shapely arms, the paler foglike thing between them which he reckoned must be her nightgown. "You should be in bed. What if Jordie wakes up?"

"Are they blaming you for it—do they think it's you?"

Fiersen shrugged. Her lips seemed to move and, bending forward a little, he heard her say, "This country's changed. Do you suppose your return could have upset something? Why do people look at you so strange?" She came nearer, trying to read his face in the gloom. "They don't like you, Jord; don't understand you. They don't want what—"

"You'd better go now, Cherry. You don't want to catch cold."

The room was chilled with the mountain air coming in through the window. He could feel it himself and he still had his clothes on. It rustled the curtains, waved the folds of her gown and ran over his face like ghostly fingers.

"Jord—" Her hand came up and again touched his arm, tightening there as, out of the night's utter silence, they heard the far-away cry of a coyote, one primitive note out of timeless space, unsettling, disturbing.

"The call of the wild," Cherry whispered, and her flesh felt cold as she pressed trembling against him. "Jord, let's get out of this?"

"How?"

"We could go away . . ."

"Too late for that."

"It is never too late! Why are you so set against leaving this place?"

"Running isn't the answer, Cherry. You can't run away from life."

"You can stay alive, anyway!"

"Is it worth that much?"

"Don't be a chivalrous fool! You can't help these people!"

"I can try," he said quietly.

She was trembling again. Her fingers dug into his arm. "I know what you think—you think it's Burr Rubelcaba! And if it is, you're crazy not to run while you can!" She said with a gust of feeling, "You're just being

169

proud and noble—you know this has gone too far to be stopped. You know there's no way you can make them believe you! I've heard what they're saying. They claim you're a night rider! They say you've built up a wild bunch—that you aim to take over this valley! You'll never talk them out of it now: and if you don't go now, you'll wind up in a noose or be shot in the back!"

"I'll not run."

"You can't stand off this whole country! They'll make you run! They'll drive you into the hills and hunt you down!"

"I reckon they'll try."

"They'll do it, too! They'll make you an outlaw . . . Oh, Jord—" she cried, "what good is pride to a dead man? Jord, don't let them—"

"There, there," Fiersen said, gently patting her shoulder. "You're letting wild thoughts upset you, Cherry. This—"

"Stop treating me like a child!" she flared. She took hold of him again and they stood like that through a disturbing silence. Her hand crept down his arm to catch hold of his fingers and she took his hand, turning the palm of it against her heart and holding it there.

He stood perfectly still, feeling the tumult

inside her. She hoped he would feel something else, something closer, that would break down the barriers and bring him to her. She was like a quick shout across wild places, completely open, wholly receptive to whatever he might have for her and, when she caught up his other hand, Fiersen saw this. She was eager, trembling, a flame in the dark with lips half parted as those wide-open eyes searched his face for expression.

He understood what she was offering; against his will felt the heat of her, felt the call of it rush all through him. She was there for him, wanting him, hungry and aching with all the lush ripe loveliness of her keyed to his slightest signal, and he knew he could never give it.

SIXTEEN

CLIFF VANCE WAS a short three miles from Bar D when he stopped his horse with a bitter oath. Fear had nothing to do with it. Just plain horse sense. The nine o'clock sun was bright and hot like the nickel part of a polished stove. Be crazy to go to Fiersen's now. He wouldn't be there. He'd be out on the range with that slanch-eyed crew.

There'd be nobody home but the cook, perhaps some chore boy. Vance had nothing to hash over with them.

He climbed off his horse and loosened the saddle. He finally turned the horse loose to browse and walked over to squat in the shade of a mesquite. What in the world had he been thinking of to come tearing over to Bar D like this? A lot of good it would do him to see Jade Fiersen . . . unless he was up to try gunning him down. If Jade had stolen those cattle, he'd hardly own up to it. Be a heap more apt to laugh in Vance's face!

Vance reckoned he had ought to be bored for the simples.

If he'd ever gone tearing into that yard and there was anyone round, he'd be too dead to skin. Of course Jade's crew had grabbed those cows! Who else would be driving stolen cattle onto Bar D range? Nobody played such tricks on Fiersen. He played for keeps.

Vance pulled his thoughts up. They were tending to travel a well worn circle. They'd covered this ground before, and much better. It was not a question of Fiersen's guilt. The real question, Vance thought, was how could they best pin it on him.

Perhaps the hunch that had fetched him

here was not so far off the mark at that. Maybe he *had* better go to Fiersen's. He'd damn sure never find a better chance. The crew would be gone with the stolen cattle. Oh, there might be three-four hands hanging close in case Jade figured to keep up appearances, but these would hardly be at the home place. And if Fiersen was there, Vance could always say he'd come over to apologize for losing his temper, for that crazy fight they'd had last night.

"Hell," Vance sighed, "there won't be nobody home. Probably won't be a damn thing suspicious; but if there should . . ."

He clapped on his hat and clanked over to his pony. It was but the work of a moment to straighten the blanket and retighten his hull. Vance was a single cinch man, and knew to a mile how much he could get out of any horse under him. He knew how to nurse a tired horse along, knew how to get that last mite of speed from one. In fifteen minutes, he was rounding a knoll and having his first bleak look at Jade's buildings.

He couldn't see the yard very well for the trees, but he saw no dust or other sign of activity. He slowed the gelding's pace to a walk and, that way, came through the thick-leaved foliage and onto the lemon-colored earth of the road. He got out the makings, rolling up a smoke as cover for the probe of wary eyes. Still fiddling with the thing, he passed the barn and came abreast of a corralful of horses that narrowed his look and turned it darker.

Those broncs had been ridden mighty hard mighty recent.

His experienced glance saw the slicked-stiff patches of dried-out sweat, the encrusted dust, general air of indifference. Blanket marks were still plain on those hides and he flung a swift look for bullet burns; and then a voice just behind him sardonically said: "Figuring to buy you a few good horses, Vance?"

Vance licked his smoke and untwisted his shoulders. He tried to appear natural as he turned around but his voice showed the jumpy pitch of his nerves; it came out edged with an irascible harshness: "Didn't know you'd lived with Indians, Calder."

"You mean I move right quick? Shucks," Calder grinned, "I expect you was doin' some powerful deep thinkin'. What you got on your mind this mornin'?"

Vance, shrugging, didn't care for the cut of Calder's stare, nor like the look of the man's smiling face. And he saw the others now spread out over the yard. Jade's fore-man observed the way his look juned around; so Vance growled, trying to make it sound jocular, "Holiday, is it?"

"No. We're just about ready to put on the nose-bag."

"My God!" Vance said. "Is it that late already?"

Calder twisted a squint at the sun. "We most generally reckon to feed about twelve. Better git down an' tie into a bite. What's new in Dry Bottom?"

"That reminds me," Vance said. "Jade around anyplace?"

"Him an' Strawn went lopin' off a couple hours ago. Gone to look at the browse up around Sheed's Mountain. I'll ride up there with you after grub if you're a mind to."

"No—no," Vance said. "I've got to get on back. Bein' over hereabouts, I just fig-ured to swap a little habla with Jade. Kinda sorry about that blow-up last night."

"You mean about your place burnin' down? We heard," Calder said, "you had quite a fire."

Vance didn't dare look at him. More and more he was regretting having come here. There was something cold and tight about the feel of this place, a stealthiness that was deviling Vance's nerves. The cook had popped out and banged on the washtub right after Calder had shot that look at the sun, but nobody yet had started for the cookshack. None of that crew had moved one inch. They were all watching Vance, and he could feel Calder watching him. Vance's collar suddenly felt too tight.

"About that burnin' you had last night," Calder prodded. "What got it started—you any idea?"

Vance hadn't known ever to have felt so cold in his life. He had to clamp his teeth to keep them from chattering.

"What's the matter with you, Vance? Don't you hear good this mornin'? Ain't comin' down with somethin', are you?"

Vance knew he'd got to say something. He understood what folly it was to sit here gawping like a fish out of water. With twitching cheeks, gone breathless with horror, eyes riveted to the crew, he heard the damning words pour out of him. "What's—what's the matter with them?"

"Them yonder?" Calder said, and laughed. "You mean them patched-up fellers? Why, Jim—that's the one with the rag round his head—got throwed by a salty bronc. That other one, Eddie, got crowded by a steer we was workin'. You know how reckless these rannies are."

Vance dragged his glance off the rag-wrapped men and forced himself to meet Calder's stare. A satanic mirth crinkled Calder's eyes. Vance could not haul his glance away. He felt stunned, unable to believe what he read in that look. All things dimmed away but those sardonic eyes, and he started a shaking hand toward his gun.

He was still like that, still shaking and reaching, when he heard the shot and fell out of his saddle.

SEVENTEEN

It WAS LATE in the afternoon of the second day after the Endite-Strawn affair at the Sparrowhawk. Taisy, waiting downstairs for the laundryman, Charley, to come back from the hotel with Frank's supper, was surprised by the amount of activity outside. The street was aburst with noise and confusion. Dust enclosed everything in a yellow pall and the horsebackers churning it up were half lost in it. Springwagons and buckboards crowded the storefronts and horses were tied all over the scene. This was not a payday night, nor was it yet night for the sun still shone through the diaphanous haze. "Whatever in the world," Taisy asked herself, "could have fetched such a scramble of men off the range?"

Nose pressed to the glass of Charley's window, she became more deeply perturbed as she watched the mounting excitement outside. Alarm clutched her heart. Surely something terrible had happened. Even through the grimed window she could hear the feverish sound of their voices, shouting and calling through the blowing dust. That crowd looked as riled as a bagful of hornets.

Taisy, biting her lips, continued to watch and tremble. All her newly won confidence was slipping away. It was like a foretaste of impending doom and she gripped the window ledge tensely as she peered at those angry passing faces.

Whatever could have happened to have loosed such an uproar? It hadn't been this bad that time Jim Wolf caught the tramp in his chicken house!

She was almost tempted to go out there; and she just might have done so except she was scared of being confronted by the lieutenant's lady, or even himself—for he was sure to be out in that devilment someplace,

178

handing down notions like they was the laws of Moses.

"Lordy, lordy!" Taisy backed from the window. She sure had no wish to be seen by them—leastways not in these clothes!

There must have been another shooting. Whoever in the world had Fiersen killed now?

Visioning the face of him, Taisy trembled anew. Such harsh unrelenting features— such awful eyes! Such a terrible man, always fighting and snarling and shooting off his pistol—it was a wonder folks stood for it! You'd think they'd be getting mighty tired of his ructions. Maybe they would if they ever got mad enough. Perhaps they were going to get mad enough this time— she purely hoped so. There must be better things in life than all this squabbling and killing. Cull that Fiersen critter out of the herd and a body could settle down to raising beef. It was all his fault—everybody said so.

She sure wished Charley would get a wiggle on. He could probably tell her what was back of this commotion; she hoped all this rumpus wouldn't disturb Frank Endite . . . Now *there* was a gentleman! Such a nice quiet feller, so refined-like and all. And so uncomplaining. Most, if they'd been shot up bad as he was, would be yelling their heads off—but not Frank. He just smiled his grave smile whenever she asked him and told her politely he was doing "just fine." But she knew dang well he must be hurting like sixty; and that sawbones wouldn't be forever coming back if his wound wasn't worse than Frank would admit to.

It just went to show the difference in fellers.

Why, there wasn't a finer galoot in Dry Bottom!

But that was the way things went in this world. It was too dang disgusting; the bad troubles always picked the finest folks to roost on. There was that bullypuss Fiersen devil raving around like a sore-back bull, stirring up things and killing every gent who had guts enough to stand his ground. Stealing people's cattle and raising hell high enough to shove a chunk under, and nobody doing a blame thing about it. It just wasn't fair! Made you think, by grab, there just wasn't no justice!

It made her boil every time she thought of poor Frank being shoved around and shot by these outlaws. And now he was going to have to go someplace else just because that Strawn hombre had claimed

Frank was cheating! Why, you'd think folks would have better sense than believe it! Take the word of a cow thief before they'd believe a decent man like Frank!

Of course Frank said they hadn't believed Strawn, and it was true that brand inspector feller had counted the deck and proved Frank honest; but just the same, Frank said, they would all be leery of him. It only took, Frank declared, just the merest suspicion to drive folks away from a gambler's table.

Trouble with Frank, he was just too open-handed, too forgiving and noble to take up for his rights. If they'd done that to *her*, she wouldn't pack up and leave; she'd stay right here and make them like it! But Frank had made up his mind; they would go some-place else and start all over.

She reckoned it might be kind of fun, at that. She hadn't ever been to no big place like Tucson or them other towns Frank had mentioned. He said she would like El Paso. Frank said in El Paso folks changed their clothes three-four times a day, and a passle of them didn't ever know their next-door neighbors! Lordy, what a place! She wasn't plumb sure she could ever get used to it. But Frank said she would and that was good enough for her.

Frank said in El Paso a lot of the houses had running water right inside of them! Frank said a heap of queer things; like, for instance, last night when she'd been fixing to red up the place. Frank said no, just leave it alone and Charley'd take care of it. "Lordy!" she'd laughed, "I can't just be a-settin' around here twiddlin' my fingers!"

"You'll have plenty to do just being a woman."

"But, lordy," she'd said, "what's bein' a woman if it ain't cleanin' and sweepin' and washin' and cookin'?"

"Servants' work!" Frank had said, lofty like.

Frank was like no one she had ever come across. So mannered and fetching, always trigged out in the latest kick of fashion. And that grin! "A woman's whole business in life," he'd explained, "can be boiled right down to one word—*decoration*. A woman's whole business is to be beautiful and fascinating, helping a man's leisure pass pleasantly. Every important woman in history has been primarily remembered because of an ability to do those things well—Sheba, Helen, Aphrodite, Cleopatra. Go right down the list," Frank declared, "and every last one of them had that knowledge and the subtle cleverness to put it to work for them. A woman should attract. You can't attract a man's interest washing dishes or sweeping."

She had shaken her head. Lord, but he was smart—sometimes she couldn't make him out at all. "So how do you go about doin' it?" she'd asked, but Frank had just grinned. "Don't worry about it. Takes time," he said. "I'll be showing you the way of it once I'm up on my feet again. Dress is a part of it; the things you wear and the way a woman wears them—there's an art to the business. Personality's part of it, manner-isms, gestures, the cadence of the voice. They're all part and parcel, even to the way a woman does her hair. The way she speaks, what she says, how she smiles, how she laughs; all these things make for charm in a woman. You've *got* personality; you can learn the rest of it. In a handful of months you can be the toast of the country."

Toast! That's just what he said. The *toast* of the country!

She shook her head again and peered through the window. Them fellers was still milling round out there, chousin' up the dust, still shouting and swearing like a corralful of mule skinners. Muttering groups of them standing all over with their heads together, faces darkly furious.

Then her glance was caught by the sight of Amos Tabbs, the old rancher from Tubac; and she flung up the window and yelled at him.

"By golly," Amos gulped, staring, "what you doin' up there, girl?"

"What's goin' on?"

"My land! Ain't you heard?"

"If I'd a-heard," Taisy said, "I wouldn't be askin' you."

"Fiersen!" Tabbs cried. "Folks is fit to be hog tied—"

"What's he done now?"

"Cut his rope too short this time! Everyone's always figgered he was back of this stealin'; now he's come right out in the open—"

"But what's he DONE?"

"Done? Boy, he's done *plenty* God only knows how many he's shot—durn fool's gone *bronc!*"

In excitable language augmented by gestures, Tabbs told the terrible news going round. Outlaws raiding clean to the Border, vandals riding the piney trails leaving death and destruction in their fiery wake. People leaving their homes all over. Main roads jammed with their pitiful traffic, the old and the lame, the palsied misfortunates who lived too far out to have any protection. He told how an old man was drowned in his cesspool, forty virgins raped and murdered between Dry Bottom and the town of Nogales.

"Strippin' the widders an' leavin' 'em naked—three kids has been found strung up by their toes! Ain't nobody safe with them owlhooters ridin'—rivers is runnin' red with blood! Feed's bein' burnt an' cattle slaughtered! Graston's sheep was set afire—gutted horses sprawled all over! They're tearin' up ranches like they was paper. Fiersen's thrown in with Curly Bill an' they're fixin' to grab off all of this country!"

Taisy trembled. "Lordy, lordy—it's the end of the world!"

"Mighty dang near, I'll tell you that. Feller's life ain't worth a plugged nickel an' them that's got women better git 'em right outa here! Amado's been raided—Carew, too, an' Proctor! Mesquite! Twin Buttes! Homesteaders bein' run out all over—you oughta hear Teke! Turkey Track's been burnt to the ground; Vance ain't been seen since yesterday mornin'—we'll hang Fiersen higher'n a kite!"

And off Tabbs went with those milling others through the growling dust toward the Sparrowhawk Bar.

A shot shook the boards of the flimsy building.

Taisy forgot about laundryman Charley. She fled through the door, white-cheeked and frantic. With shaking hands and stumbling steps, she came panting up the outside stairs and flung open Frank's door.

Stopped, aghast, on the threshold, nearly swooning. Frank was half off the bed trying to get himself up. There was blood all over the front of his shirt.

Through a miasma of horror, Taisy stood there speechless, her stare flashing across the sun-bathed ledge of the open window, eyes fixed on the stubby ends of eight grubby fingers clamped to the outside edge of the sill.

And then they were gone with a slither of sound.

She ran to the window. It was sound released her, bent her head out the window—the sound of that dropping body landing on bootheels. And suddenly she saw him, running, making for a horse by the alder thicket, a horse with a Bar D brand on its hip.

The man's back was toward her; she got no look at his face.

But she remembered the clothes. They were the things Jade Fiersen had worn in the Sparrowhawk the night his range boss had accused Strawn of cheating. Still with his face turned away from her, the man's arm snaked out and caught up the reins. The horse was going full tilt when he got into the saddle. Drumming hoofs swiftly carried him from sight.

A groan from Endite pulled her back from the window. Frank was on his feet, staggering. His face was ghastly, clammed with sweat, and his eyes were rolling. His knees gave way just before she could get to him and he fell face down across the carpetless floor.

One word sighed out of his twisted lips. "Fiersen—"

That was all.

He died with his head in her arms.

EIGHTEEN

THE SPARROWHAWK BAR was packed to the doors. Every able-bodied man in the town of Dry Bottom not too drunk to get around was wedged in there. They were all packing guns and a lot of them looked to be aching to use them. The air was rank and charged with impatience and smelled pretty strong of horses and sweat. No drinks filled the gnarled and rope-scarred fists, no charity shone from perspiring faces. They were here to determine how to stop Jade Fiersen.

And Burr Rubelcaba was ready to tell them.

He stood six feet in his high-heeled boots with a muscular swell of neck and shoulders. White teeth gleamed in his round dark face, bold and lively features flushed with the anger of a righteous man.

"If a feller come along and put his boot in your belly, I expect you would knock him hell west and crooked. But if six galoots come along all together, you might feel some puzzled which to poke first. That's how it is here; that's what we're up against," Rubelcaba told them.

"We say it's Fiersen back of this shootin', stealin' and burnin'. Some figures it's him and Curly Bill teamed together—but we don't *know* a damn thing about it. We don't even know—now hold on a minute; I'll do the talkin'. We don't *know*, I say, that it's Fiersen, Curly Bill or anybody else. Alls we're doin' is guessin'. Now we don't want to do some fool thing we'll be sorry for. If Fiersen's guilty, he'll be punished; what we want right now is a handful of facts. Rumors right now is twenty to the dozen. We don't want rumors. We're after *facts*. Before I go bendin' my gun on somebody—"

He broke off and stood back with those hard pale eyes bleakly blazing with temper. When the uproar had quieted, he let a gusty breath fall out of him and declared with a stiff-necked arrogance: "If any of you rannies got a mind to take over, just step right up here—be all right with me. I never did shine at this jaw-waggin' no way. You there, Patch—come up here an' talk to 'em!"

Patch grinned ruefully and stayed in his tracks. "You're doin' all right," he mumbled; and somebody else, with half a laugh, swore. "Was it facts you said?"

Rubelcaba, giving them a hard look, nodded. "Makes a lot of difference who's back of this ruckus. If it's somebody else, we don't want to smash Fiersen—"

"Ain't doubtin' it's Fiersen, are you?"

"What I think an' what the law might come up with could mighty easy be two different things. We don't want to be startin' anything we can't finish. Any of you got any proof against Fiersen?"

Teke pulled back his lips in a sneer. This was Vance's Turkey Track foreman, hard-nosed and ugly. "You know any rustlin' son of a bitch that would have enough guts to shove stole cattle onto Bar D range without they was plumb in cahoots with Jade?" Sneering again, he spat. "That herd of ours went straight to Fiersen's an' I say, by Gawd, that's proof enough for me!"

This appeared to be the general consensus of opinion. Joe Moses said, "Same bunch struck my place that went through Schrae-der's—six of the bastards. All ridin' Bar D horses."

And one of the Baker boys declared, "Since when has Fiersen ever rented out horseflesh?" and somebody tittered.

" 'Course it's Fiersen," Teke snarled bit-terly. "Nobody but a fool would ever think different!"

"Just the same," Rubelcaba decided, "that still ain't proof that'll stand before the law. Them broncs could have been stolen. Easi-est thing in the world. Jade runs his stuff on the open range. Anyone wantin' to shove a spoke in his wheel could've rounded up some of his horses an' used 'em—I could've done it myself. We got to have proof that'll stand up in court."

"Court!" Teke howled, and a number of others took up the same cry. These man weren't hot for that sort of justice; what they wanted was revenge—real personal. They wanted to see Fiersen at the end of a rope, and they wanted both hands on that rope in addition.

Rubelcaba said bluntly: "There's two ways of doin' this, the right an' the wrong way. We put Dave Blankenstraw into office to uphold our rights an' to keep law an' order. I'm for takin' this to him an' havin' it done right. If Fiersen's guilty, Dave'll see he gets all that's comin' to him, an' we won't be standin' with our pants around our ankles."

Through the angered growls, Jim Tarlton, the Tucson brand inspector, spoke up. "Burr's right. Like he always is. Any bunch of hotheads can hustle out and hang a man— a damn good way to get your own necks stretched. Thing to do is get behind our sheriff and see that he gets all the help he'll be needin'. While you might not think we've much law in these parts, we won't ever have any if we don't uphold it. Let's listen to Burr, now, and—"

191

"You're a fool!" Teke said with contempt. "Things has come to a fine pass, I say, when the Santa Cruz Valley's got to call in help to wash out a little dirt off its doorstep!"

Rubelcaba's cold eye went over Teke like the rasp of a file. "What I suggest binds no man, but it's the only move we can make that has any real chance of ironing out this situation. My suggestion is this: Elect two-three fellers to speak for us; send 'em to Tucson an' put the facts before the sheriff. As a public servant, it's his duty to help us—"

"An' that'll be the end of it!" Teke sneered.

"At least," Tarlton said, "we'll have done our part. If the sheriff continues to rest his boots on a desk top, we can still take the law into more violent hands, I reckon. I recollect you tried to get tough once before hereabouts; you strung up Stack Aiken an' what did it get you? Come out later, he never took them horses. Had Stack been a big rancher like Fiersen, some of you gents would still be makin' small rocks out of big ones at Yuma. Better think this over before you wake up with rewards on your noggins. I'd be sorry to see—"

"That damn sheriff won't git outa his chair!" Teke yelled. "I've known that feller for the past ten years an' I've yet to see him arrest anyone that wasn't sleepin' it off in some gutter! While he's hemmin' an' hawin', we'll be drove plumb outa here!"

Rubelcaba stood back and folded his arms while waiting for them to get it out of their systems. Tarlton said, "If Dave is such a poor shakes, why'd you elect him? You voted for him, Granly—you did, too, Patch—"

"Yeah. So did Jade Fiersen!" Teke shouted through the uproar. "An' all the gamblers an' pimps, an' killers an' rustlers from here to Nogales! You'll see, by Gawd! Alls he'll do is set on his tail an' tell you there just ain't nothin' he *can* do about it!"

"All right, Teke," Rubelcaba said. "What do you allow we should do?"

"Hang him, by Gawd—an' the quicker the better!"

"I nominate you to catch him and take care of it."

"I'll second the motion," Tarlton said, curt with temper. "You want to turn this country into a slaughter pen, hop to it! *I* don't have to live here—nor stay here, either. Start up a range war if that's what you're achin' fer."

Some of the racket began to simmer down. In this uncomfortable limelight, Teke slanched an uneasy look around. "I—" He broke off, jaw sagging, the rest of him suddenly, rigidly still. A whisper of escaping breath came out of him and heads all over the room began turning.

Between the wedged-back batwings of the Sparrowhawk's entrance, a man stood with his thumbs hooked over a gun belt. Dust powdered his clothes and grimed the lines of his taciturn features. There was nothing of menace in the newcomer's attitude unless one counted his silence, yet sweat was plain on Teke's livid face, and in the quiet about him you could have heard a gnat sigh.

"I understand," Fiersen said, "you'd like to stop this rustling."

Sweat built a sheen on a number of other faces. It seemed the crowd scarcely breathed. "Have you decided what to do?" Fiersen asked Rubelcaba.

"It's been my suggestion," the Spanish Cross owner stated, "that we take it up with the sheriff."

Fiersen nodded. "Sounds like a move in the right direction. Before you do anything, I've a couple remarks I'd like to pass on.

First I'd like you to know I'm not rustling anybody's cows."

A wildness threaded the air and was felt. Obe Mailstell blinked his black lashless eyes. The Baker boy's face got darkly angry and Joe Moses shifted his weight with a solemn care. Like a rising wind, you could feel their hate piling up, strengthening, slithering its tentacles out through the crowd. And you could see it take hold in the stiffening shoulders and tightening mouths. You could almost hear it in the rasp of their breathing.

Fiersen put one arm against the doorframe, watching.

"You fools," he said. "One of the biggest steals in the country is due to come off right before your damned eyes and you can't see anybody back of it but me. Take a look at how it might be if one man owned the whole of this valley; that's the picture one of your friends has up his sleeve. And all he needs to make it come true is to furnish a scapegoat to hold your attention while he's whittling you down."

A bottle-brown flash from the dying sun struck a bright shine from the green eyes watching them. A tight little smile tugged the edges of his mouth as he tapped out a measure on the doorframe with his fingers and Rubelcaba gave him a narrower scrutiny and Teke's stare shifted to Rubelcaba.

"So I'm set up for the scapegoat," Fiersen drawled, "and everyone seems mighty well suited."

He stood there at ease, a yellow haired man with an arm on the doorframe and his two booted feet planted firmly under him. "You might just as well settle down and forget it."

"Fergit what?" said old Tabbs, looking muddled.

"What the whole tinhorn bunch of you are holding your breath for. Ain't nobody going to be that foolish. Unless," he smiled thinly, "our friend who's bamboozling the bunch of you cares to be heard on the subject."

It got considerably quieter.

Once again Joe Moses carefully shifted his weight; and Jim Tarlton said softly, "Guess I'll go home."

"Guess again," Fiersen told him. "You've got an interest in this. Better stick around."

"We've heard enough of your bullshit," Teke grumbled roughly. "We know who's behind what's happenin' here—you an' your wild bunch of cow-stealin' butchers!" He came a step forward, one hand clamped to his pistol. "You're the one back of this! You're . . ."

His voice cracked and quit. He let go of the pistol to throw a hand out before him as though to ward off something read in Fiersen's stare.

But Fiersen still leaned on the doorframe, unmoving. "Why don't you yank that thing and have done with it?"

Teke had certainly had that intention in mind. A moment ago he had thought to do so; the look of that intention had been written all over him. The will to shoot Fiersen had been fiercely in him but now all he wished was to get himself out of this. His knees started shaking, but that brash gust of courage that had jumped him forward was a gone, withered thing, leaked away in the moisture that was filming his cheeks. His shape was still crouched; he didn't dare straighten it. Not again would he have touched that pistol for anything.

Fiersen's stare had stopped him in his tracks, punctured his bravado, left him ludicrous. No one else found anything but a frigid complacence in the look Fiersen bent on him.

"That's right," Fiersen murmured, seeing the Turkey Track man elevating his arms. "Grab ahold of your ears. Now tell us where Vance was the last time you saw him."

Several times Teke licked at dry lips without finding his voice. Then he said with the sound of a gate hinge skreaking, "Yesterday mornin' in Blakely's west pasture. Headin' for your place."

"Yeah? Well, he never turned up at Bar D—"

"That's *your* story." Rubelcaba leaned forward. "I'm not the man to jump at conclusions; but I'll say, Fiersen, I don't believe it."

"Since you're talking, for the record, where do you reckon Vance is?"

"It's my guess he's dead, buried on your place or mighty close by!" Rubelcaba said loudly; and all over that room men's hands reached hipward.

NINETEEN

As FRANK ENDITE had guessed, Taisy Aiken was just a green kid from the back of beyond, malleable, without experience, ripe for most anything. Born of a self-centered floozy and sired by a whisky guzzling horse-thieving father, she had grown as a weed without care or comfort, a child of the hills, reared by wind, rain and storm.

Just eighteen, come this year's grass, with barely enough schooling to read, rather slowly, and to write after a fashion. Reading matter at Stack Aiken's tarpaper shanty had been mostly limited to tinned food labels, one dog-eared copy of the leather-bound *Twelve Months Volunteer*, and mail order catalogues which disappeared sheet by sheet with the days, though old Rufus Kinchley, the Santa Cruz sky-pilot, had on his infrequent visits generally dropped off a book or two in the hope of endowing her with wider horizons. Notwithstanding Stack's jibes and sneers, she had read painstakingly such weighty tomes as *The Horse & Dog* by H. Sample, *The Golden State: A History of the Region West of the Rocky Mountains*, Peters' *Kit Carson's Life and Adventures*, and *A Student's History of the American People, with a Texas Supplement*, which she had worked her way through more from a sense of duty than with any great degree of enthusiasm.

None of these things offered much solace as she stared down into Frank's dead face. "It's just like somethin' were a-twistin' my heart out," she cried with a shudder. "It ain't right—it purely ain't fittin' that a fine square gent like Frank should be took off this way without a chance. I ort to be a-cryin' for him but I just can't seem to do it. . . . I reckon I'm a-carin' too much for tears."

She suspected the tears would come when she'd got more used to his loss. She could not rightly comprehend it yet; it was too plumb awful to contemplate. "All them grand things we was fixin' to do . . . all them marvelous places he were a-goin' to show me. Oh, Frank!" she cried, and the tears came at last as she buried her face against Frank's shoulder.

What had she to live for? Dreary years stretching away interminably. All was insecurity and doubt. Nothing to hope for, nothing to cherish but poor Frank's memory; no sunlight, no laughter; all snatched away by that assassin's bullet. No laces, no jewels, no silks and no satins. She cried as much for the dreams denied her as she did for the author of those glib promises; a bereaved and desolate woman with no comparisons by which she might know what a poor imitation of a man Frank had been. She knew only a terrible emptiness.

She guessed she ought to go off and drown herself; tortured souls, she'd been told, often did such things. Could she ever forget his exciting glances? the caress of his voice? that tingling uncertainty of living here with him? *Living in sin*—that was what she'd been doing. And this was what came of it. God had snatched him away. God had sent Jade Fiersen to punish her.

A horrid thought she felt, shivering.

Yet how could she doubt it?

She remembered those fingers gripping the ledge just before Frank's killer had dropped to the ground. She remembered the horse he had run for whose hip had been scarred with Jade Fiersen's brand; she'd seen him ride off toward Jade Fiersen's ranch. Though she had not caught a glimpse of his face, by those fingers she would know him, by that horse, and those clothes he'd had on him that night in the Sparrowhawk. It was Fiersen, all right—with his dying breath Frank had called him Fiersen.

She would never forget the look of those fingers grubbily hooked to the window ledge in that horrible interval before he'd let go. She remembered each crack and crevice, the look of his skin and the cuticle even; and by these things she would prove it against him.

Frank had known him, she recalled Frank mentioning him even before gasping Fiersen's name as he died. They had known each other before at some place called The Siding. Taisy tried to call up what Frank had told her about it, but with her thoughts churning round like they were, she couldn't. Seemed like Jade Fiersen and killing went as purely together as pistols and bullets. Lordy! That was it—*gunman!* That was what Frank had called him. *A flip-and-shoot gunslinger!* And something about ketchup.

Tenderly she lowered Frank's head to the floor, having to bite her lips to keep back the tears. Never again would she hear Frank's deep laugh, not ever again would he hold her spellbound with the wonder of tales he could spin of far places, and those fifty cent words she had never understood. It came over her oddly how ignorant she was, and she was suddenly frightened. What was she doing here? What was she waiting for? These rooms had always seemed a sanctuary; she had thought them the friendliest rooms in the world. But now all the good was gone out of them. They seemed cold and drab and rough and shabby and there was no friendliness in them. What if Charley came up with their suppers and saw Frank? Would he imagine she had killed him?

She looked around wildly. With her heart

pounding, she jumped to her feet filled with dread and alarm. Why, they might even hang her!

But with her hand on the door, she stopped again. With sagging shoulders, she lurched back to the bed and sank down on it. Why should she care what they did with her?

She hid her face in her hands. Another thought came and she snatched them away. Lordy! what kind of woman was she, crying around like old Biddy Stephens! Frank hadn't liked crying women—he'd said so. He said crying was for kids, and he was probably right.

Taisy dabbed at her eyes with the hem of her skirt. She had ought to be thinking of Frank, not herself. Of poor Frank lying there dead on the floor . . . dead of a bushwhacker's bullet. Lordy! Sniveling over the wreck of her life and letting Frank's killer get clean away—what must Frank think of her!

Taisy blushed with the heat of shame.

Frank would want his killer brought to justice. Whereat was her mind to be letting that gunfighter get away like she had!

She pushed herself up. "Never mind,

Frank," she told his dead face, "I'll take care of it . . . I'll be a-killin' him for you."

She would need a gun. Much as she would like to, she couldn't kill Fiersen with plain bare hands. She would have to have a gun and she would have to find him. She would do it, too! She would find him if it took all the rest of her life!

Frank did not wear a gunbelt or holster but she guessed he must have a gun on him someplace. She would have to go through his pockets unless—her glance flashed to Frank's bags underneath the bed. She pulled them out, a scratched-up suitcase and a smaller dog-eared hand bag—Frank had called it a Gladstone. She got them open, went through them carefully without finding a weapon. There were a lot of packs of unopened playing cards, some laundered shirts, two cravats and some underwear; but no pistol.

Replacing Frank's things, she closed the bag, seeing how scuffed and shabby they looked and thinking of all those far places they'd been. There was a tear in the hide of the smaller one like it had been dragged across something sharp and ragged. She patted it with a forlorn affection, thinking how long and how well it had served him.

Straightening, she went over again to look down on Frank's body, remembering how he'd got up off the bed with sweat all over his pain-wracked face, how he'd stood there swaying, trying to tell her about it. And the remembered sound of his voice gasping "Fiersen—" and how he had clutched at his side and fallen. Seemed almost as though he'd been reaching for something. Had she read this wrong? He still had the hand half inside a vest pocket—could he have been trying to say he'd something inside that pocket for Fiersen?"

Frowning, very carefully she lifted Frank's hand out. There was something white clutched in Frank's dead fingers—a paper. A little white envelope, crumpled and twisted. She smoothed it out on her knee, trying to make out the name Frank had written there. The writing was blurred but the name wasn't Fiersen; it was something or other Carver.

"Sure he wouldn't," she thought, "be meanin' it for Fiersen—it was Fiersen killed him."

She jumped up, frantic. Someone was shouting at the foot of the steps. A man's voice, impatient. Calling for Endite.

Taisy looked around wildly. Suppose he

came up here! She thrust Frank's envelope into the tear on the Gladstone bag and hurried to the door; already pounding feet were on their way up.

Catching hold of the door, she opened it enough to poke out her head. A scowling cowboy stood just below her. "He isn't here," she cried. "Frank's not here!"

The man eyed her curiously. "Then where the—where is he?"

"Not here," Taisy said.

The fellow appeared minded to look for himself.

"Go away," Taisy muttered. "I'm not decent—I'm dressin'."

"Well, you tell him they're wantin' him down at the Sparrowhawk. Tell him Slocum says for him to git right over there."

Taisy pulled back her head, hastily closing the door. Locked it and leaned there, weak, her knees shaking.

Her sigh was an outpouring rush of breath. "Whew!" she cried faintly, and went back to Frank. Found a fat-barreled derringer in one of his pockets. Laying it on the bed, she got up and went to the built-in closet where Frank kept his suits. Found three pairs of pants and three sets of boots. She guessed Frank must have liked his boots tight; she stamped her feet into them and pulled off her dress and the petticoat under it. Then she pulled on a pair of Frank's pants.

They'd do, she guessed, with the legs stuffed down inside the boot tops. But what in the world could she put on for a shirt? None of Frank's would even come near fitting. She stared back at the dress she'd dropped on the floor. Went over and got it. Picking it up she looked wistfully down at the soft blue material, feeling its goodness with reverent fingers. She would have to do it, she purely would—she couldn't go riding around half naked!

She felt thankful she didn't have on that terrible corset. She'd been mighty relieved when Frank had said only fat ladies wore them, that she looked better natural. She felt better anyhow. Lordy, lordy.

She looked again at the precious goods in her hands, at this dress a lieutenant had bought for his lady. Shutting her eyes, she prayed for strength and then, straightaway while the prayer was fresh, took a firm hold of the dress at the hem and ripped the skirt up the seam to the waist, then around the waist till the skirt fell free. And she had her shirt, sort of a blouse, which she tucked inside Frank Endite's pants. Getting out one of his fancy vests, she put that on, hoping it might hide her bulges a little, letting it flap like the cowboys did.

Back to the bed she picked up Frank's derringer and hunted the darkening room for a hat, but all she found was Frank's silk tile. Which wouldn't be a whole heap of good on a horse but she took it anyway, bunching her red hair into its crown. Might help for the moment to disguise her identity. She sure didn't want to be stopped short of Fiersen's.

Recollecting her money, she went and fetched it and let herself nervously out of the door. With pounding heart, she stood on the landing and peered through the dusk at the empty street. It was not empty, really. Stamping and tail-switching horses were all over the place and wagons and buckboards still cluttered the store fronts, but nowhere was there any sign of a person. Where had they got to? Whereat was all that great bunch of ranch hands?

Tightly gripping the railing, Taisy moved hesitantly down the steps.

At the bottom, she stopped. Originally she'd planned to go to Riggs' stable and demand a horse. Foreseeing difficulties, she had counted on Endite's name to help; she'd meant to say she was borrowing it for Frank.

But now that notion didn't look so good. Suppose Mister Riggs wasn't partial to Frank! Or wondered why Frank didn't come his own self!

Better not risk it. Plenty of horses right here for the taking, better ones probably than she'd get from the stable. And no questions asked.

The light was swiftly fading now. Night would soon roll over the land. She must get away. She must hurry . . .

A roughening wind shouldered past her dismally.

She ran to the nearest hitchrack and clung there, her stare wildly probing the shadows. Everything looked so strange and unlikely. Even the dusty fronts of the buildings appeared to be watching her, passing judgment. No suppertime smoke crawled out of the chimneys, no clink and clank from the hoof-shaper's hammer came to enliven this sinister quiet. Beyond the last shack, the land stretched interminably, dun and drear, to the faraway peaks of those yonder mountains. Save for the horses she seemed to be alone, one more ghost in a phantom town.

Her legs felt suddenly weak as water. "I

got to," she muttered. "I *got* to! Poor Frank's a-countin' on me to avenge him. He'll not rest easy if I don't go out there and kill Jade Fiersen."

She peered at the stone colored sky to the north where the skyline merged with those dark smudged peaks. Glance still sweeping the deserted street, with a growing sense of apprehension, she scanned the shifting shadows for movement.

"I just *got* to!" she muttered fiercely, and crept around to the closest horse. "Sho' now—sho' now. I ain't a-goin' to hurt you." The nervous horse sidled with cocked ears, warily watching as she unloosed his reins from the tie rail. He stepped a little away from her then as though he would test the strength of her purpose. She drew him back, reaching the reins up around his neck, gripping the horn with them caught in her hand. "Sho' now," she murmured, and swung into the saddle.

The horse blew through his nose and trembled a little, but let her back him out onto the road. She still had Frank's tile on her head, hair stuffed up into it. She hadn't any spurs but, jamming the hat down firm as she might, she pounded both heels against the animal's ribs.

The excited horse took off with a will. *Cloppety-cloppety-clop-clop-clop* came the sound of his hoofs rolling off the dark buildings. She gave him his head and they went like thunder past the last shack and over the bridge and off through the dust of the valley trail.

This was a sweet-running horse, alert and with savvy, and a natural gait that seemed at least hopeful to the female person clamped on his back. She relaxed a trifle, pulled off Frank's hat and let the good wind blow wild through her hair. She threw up her head and drew night's smell deep into her soul and, for a while, was content to just leave everything up to her mount.

Some of the tenseness, the nervous strain, eased up a bit. A feeling of release flowed exultantly through her from out of the rhythm of the bay's pounding hoofs. The flow of motion, the wind in her face, took her back to childhood days when, all by herself on the back of old Charlie, she had roved all over this tawny country. Frank Endite's vest whipped and flapped in the breeze and the bay's powerful quarters rose and fell and the dark all around got steadily deeper.

Then, of a sudden, she pulled the horse

up, all that new-found confidence departing. From behind, far back where pinpricks of light marked the shape of Dry Bottom, came the racketing crash of gunfire, faint but tumultuous, dim and urgent, quickening every nerve in her body.

Her heart stood still, the breath caught in her throat. With a strangled cry, she flung herself forward and beat at the bay with her dead man's boots.

Later, much later, she stopped again. The night masked practically everything around her. She caught the vague shapes of old gnarled trees, a farther dense blotch of luminous black which she guessed must be hills, but nothing familiar was really discernible. She'd been raised in this country, had thought she knew it, but could not recognize where she was.

She got off the bay, staring about her uncertainly. She gripped the reins tightly, probing the murk to right and left. "Lordy!" she whispered, staring behind her. There, against the lesser dark of the night, she glimpsed the bulk of Mount Fagan, but so jumbled and smudged and changed was all else, the great upthrust crag confused her the more, and she cried despairingly "Lordy, where am I?"

There should have been a drift fence along about here but she failed to find it. Leading the bay, she tramped back and forth, becoming more and more upset and by this increasing the unrest of the horse. If she could not find that dratted fence, she'd be lost for sure.

Perhaps it was farther back in the brush. She wished there'd been a moon or something. The sky was completely overcast; not so much as one star could she see. There was nothing at all to provide a direction.

She tried again to orient herself in relation to the mountain, but this was small help without something more and she began then to wonder if it *was* Mt. Fagan she was peering at. It did seem to look a little like Huerfano Butte. "God, don't let it be Huerfano," she thought. Huerfano Butte was miles from her objective. Away beyond the Bar D ranch house.

Another notion suddenly assailed her. She'd no idea whose horse this was; had not thought to look for a brand. What if it was one of Rubelcaba's! A horse turned loose to find its own way invariably heads for home. She could not remember if she'd tried to guide this critter. She'd started off right coming away from Dry Bottom but couldn't, to save her, recall if she'd held him toward Fiersen's. She had been so busy with her wretched thoughts.

If she could make out the big bay's brand, she reckoned she might have some notion of where she was.

Keeping a good tight hold on the reins, she swung off, walking down the animal's length until she could get a hand on his hip. But the hide was smooth, there was no brand on it.

Maybe it was on the other hip. Once she knew whose it was, she could let him take her back where he'd come from; but first she'd better learn where that was, it being quite in the cards she'd not want to go there. She'd no desire to find herself in Tubac, or Proctor, or Amado, or any of those other towns close to the border. She'd as soon find herself at Huerfano.

Ducking under her mount's head, she started down his off side but the bay appeared suddenly to have had enough of it, sidling away. When she persisted, he began to act up, showing more perverseness than her attempt to move down the wrong side should account for. He kept flinging up his head, crab-stepping nervously, blowing through his nostrils.

"Now, now," Taisy soothed. "Whoa, now, *whoa!*" She led him around several times in a tight circle but this didn't improve things much. She bit her lip in vexation. "Whoa, boy—whoa!"

Their gyrations had taken them close to some brush but Taisy, intent on her purpose, paid no attention; the horse was cutting up frantically now. He seemed beside himself—even in this darkness she could feel his excitement; she glimpsed his rolling eyes, those laid-back ears; he was almost squatting, so hard was he endeavoring to break loose of her hold. What if he got away! It was all she could do just to hang onto him. Quivering with fright, he had his head away up and she could not get it down. He suddenly threw all his weight against the stretched reins. They burned through her hands.

With a loud squeal of terror, he was abruptly free of her and Taisy, off balance, felt herself hurtling backwards. Brush snapped, its thorny claws ripping through her clothing as she sank floundering into it. Then she heard it—that sudden harsh rattle. Something struck her leg just above the boot top.

TWENTY

Taisy lay a long time without moving, paralyzed with dread.

Fear, at first, had convulsed her muscles. She could hardly believe a snake had struck her; all her life she had lived in this country and never before had one even threatened her. But when cold sweat spread its clammy fingers, she knew she was bitten.

Stunned by the awful impact of it she lay, damp and shaking, in a kind of stupor. She'd never considered being hit by a rattler. They'd been so all-fired common she had never even thought of them. The unreality of actually being struck even now seemed almost too unlikely for credulity. She stared at the sky through the dark dusty foliage, wondering if she were dreaming. She began to feel nauseated and panic grabbed her. Scrambling up, wild with terror, she ran from the brush.

But not far. When she realized what she was doing she stopped. Folks said you had better not move much after being snake struck. The rank injustice of the whole thing angered her and she cried out bitterly. "The damn wrigglin' sneak!"

The ridiculous side of calling names at a snake wrenched a wan smile out of her, but she'd very little doubt how truly desperate her situation was. This was not a region or a time to auger much likelihood of somebody coming along and finding her—certainly not soon enough to do her much good. She'd seen people die from rattlesnake venom and knew if she didn't get help mighty soon . . . and remembered, then, that the leg would swell; that she'd better be getting her boot off.

She sat down and tugged at it. Already the leg was beginning to bloat. Several times she thought to hear the rumor of a traveling horse, but if there was a horse out there it was probably the one she'd stolen in Dry Bottom. But *he* wasn't likely to be hanging around! Just the same, she stubbornly refused to give up hope.

Again she tried to think what to do. She hadn't much time; there wasn't nobody tough enough to throw off a thing like this, though she did recollect one of her father's horses being bit on the nose and going right on about its business. But, drat it all, she wasn't no horse!

A strange lassitude was beginning to steal over her, threatening to submerge all her natural initiative. It was the poison working, spreading through her bloodstream. She ought to have cut the fang marks open but she had no knife, nothing sharp enough to cut with.

Maybe the sight on Frank's pistol . . . She suddenly found herself sobbing, and that roused her anger. Hell, everyone had to die sometime! It sure wouldn't help none to sit here sniveling—she knew what Frank thought of a sniveling woman. But Frank— oh, lord! Poor Frank was dead, a-laying in his blood on that cold carpetless floor; and this recalled to her mind how she came to be out here, and reckoned she was going to be too late for that.

"Jest a snivelin' woman," she groaned with a shudder.

But not even that would fetch her up off the ground.

She dug a big handkerchief out of Frank's pocket and blew her nose. And that didn't help a great deal either.

She gingerly touched the swelling leg and, in a shivering terror, tugged the pantsleg up and touched the burning, bloated flesh. "Reckon you're a goner, right enough," she muttered. "Reckon you ain't a-goin' to settle with no one."

If only she'd something she could tie round the leg . . . "A turnaquit might anyways slow it down some . . ." She recollected Frank's handkerchief still in her hand, tried to tug the pantsleg higher but the dang thing just wouldn't stretch no farther. Maybe she'd ought to pull the dratted pants off— "Lordy, no!" she cried. Whatever was she about to think of such a thing! She wasn't going to have folks a-finding her like that. Dead with her pants off! Lordy, lordy!

Pulling off Frank's belt, she strapped that around the leg, just above where the snake had hit her. She yanked the belt just as tight as she could and hung grimly onto it.

She supposed she had ought to get moving somewhere, and twisted around, hoping to see her horse. She guessed he was probably halfway home. A fit of shuddering seized her. She bent over and retched, soaking with sweat. Her skin felt clammy. She was burning up. With her eyes rolling wildly, she broke into a harsh laugh. The shadows round her were fuzzy like great black caterpillars, creeping and crawling and, abruptly, one of them, a crazy long-headed critter with teeth, began snorting and shying away from her, for all the world, she thought, like a nervous horse. Then it broke apart and the part on the ground came over and touched her.

"My God, it's alive—it's a woman, Ginger!"

TWENTY-ONE

THE MASS MEETING of the ranchers broken up by Fiersen's pistol had been called by Rubelcaba as an integral part of the master plan by which he had anticipated firmly seating himself in the power structure saddle. Power, in his mind, was control of the Santa Cruz Valley. An ambitious concept certainly, and one few men could hope to realize in the span of a natural lifetime. Rubelcaba had seen the priorities clearly. Having pulled himself up by his bootstraps, he saw no reason why he should not soon find the goal in plain sight.

Born of a drunken wedlock between an impoverished itinerant lawyer and a brazen-eyed bordertown hussy, Rubelcaba was the product of the place and time; bold, unscrupulous, plausible and confident. Both edgy and reckless, all opposing qualities were melded by acuteness of vision, sly perception, an agile mind sharply honed by cunning.

Fiersen, by his plan, should be the whipping boy. Neighbor must be roused against neighbor, all of them prejudiced against this formidable cow-stealing gunslinger, Fiersen. He was determined Fiersen should reap the villain's fate.

Through Teke, he'd moved Vance around at will. Calder, Fiersen's foreman, and Tarlton, the Tucson brand inspector, were the key men on whom he depended to circulate rumors and spike opposition. These were the dupes who would insure his success, and a share in the spoils should bind their loyalty.

Fiersen's unexpected entrance on the meeting at the Sparrowhawk had been, he felt, a very pleasant surprise. At every turn the bullheaded fool played into his hands; the fellow's directness would yet be the death of him—yes, Rubelcaba would see to that. Though there'd been no one hurt by that gunplay, all those dumb ranchers believed Fiersen had started it. The man's main wish had been simply to get away; it had taken quick thinking on Rubelcaba's part to tilt tempers sufficiently to permit the man to do so. He'd *wanted* Fiersen out; he did not want Jade Fiersen killed yet. Fiersen must be saved for the flaming finale, for the coup bound to follow Fiersen's flight to the hills. Lost in those arroyos and gulches, hounded and hunted, Fiersen would reap the blame for each bit of villainy done in this valley.

Rubelcaba had laid his plans well. Slank Calder had been the original rustler, Calder and the men he had put on Jade's payroll. Discovering this, Rubelcaba had brought him into the plan. Teke, with a few of Vance's Turkey Track crew, had also been lured by easy pickings; and that brand inspector, Tarlton, had been right there when dollars talked.

The stolen cattle were another neat touch, being openly sold at Tucson's stock yards. Tarlton, inspecting them, found nothing wrong with the increasing stream of brand-vented cattle being sold under the aegis of the Bar D foreman. Rubelcaba figured that, when—as must eventually happen—these transactions were inevitably discovered, they would brand Jade Fiersen irrevocably as a rustler. Calder, then, would turn state's evidence and clinch the lies beyond dispute.

Rubelcaba, of course, was leaning heavily on the unlikelihood of Fiersen ever coming to trial; but if he should, Calder could be depended on to apply the finishing touches.

Yes, it was shaping up well. Fiersen was still on the loose, to be sure. But before that meeting at the Sparrowhawk disintegrated, Joe Moses, Amos Tabbs and Rubelcaba himself had been appointed a committee of three to present the ranchers' grievances to the sheriff at Tucson. They were to head for that place first thing in the morning. If the sheriff refused to be moved by their prodding—if he wouldn't send deputies to Dry Bottom, hell would pop in no small fashion.

Rubelcaba, now on his way to Cottonwood Seep, allowed himself a couple of sly chuckles. If he knew Sheriff Blankenship, hell would pop high, wide and handsome.

Arrived at the Seep, he moved into the trees' deep shadows and waited.

Climbing down off his horse, he loosened the saddle, reins trailed so his mount wouldn't stray but be free, if he cared to, to crop at the grass which along this sheltered way was knee deep.

He did not have very long to wait. Inside of ten minutes the Bar D foreman, Slank Calder, joined him. Plainly Calder's thoughts were not salubrious. An uneasy edginess was stamped in the cut of his shoulders. It was in the guarded look of his glance as he frittered his mount across the path of the moon, at once backing the animal into deep shadow.

"You're hard on a horse," Rubelcaba observed. "Get off the dumb brute and give him a rest."

"Hard!" You could almost hear Calder's chin whip up. "Hard, says you!" and swore softly, wickedly, under his breath.

Rubelcaba chuckled. "You got any notion where Fiersen is now?"

"He was headed for town last I seen of him."

Rubelcaba lit and with much comfort puffed at his stogie, letting the good smoke drift through his nostrils, savoring the warm scented smell of it. "Came into the meetin'. Had himself quite a gunbending time. Wanted to know where Vance was, and I told him—"

Calder wheeled his horse full around. "What you tryin' to do—get me killed?"

Rubelcaba's head was shrouded in smoke.

"By God!" Calder swore, "I don't like it! You'd no call to—"

"I was makin' the play for the crowd, not

for Jade. Anyhow, he won't be havin' no chance to find him, so he'll not know whether I was lyin' or not. Here's what you do: drop a few hints I been askin' around who's the father of that kid his housekeeper's got. That'll keep his mind off Vance for awhile. Calls the kid Jordie, don't she?"

Calder's horse backed into deeper dark. Rubelcaba grinned. "Still touchy about it, are you? Ain't you noticed that fluff Frank Endite's picked up? Now there's a gal—"

"Shh!" Calder hissed; and they bent forward, listening.

"Teke or Tarlton," Rubelcaba grunted. "Told 'em to meet us here. We'll be layin' pipe for the windup tonight."

Horse sound could be heard moving steadily nearer, Teke's bull shape abruptly showing in the moonlight and, behind him, Tarlton's.

Yards away both men reined up, closely studying the shadows.

"That hombre wouldn't trust his own mother," Rubelcaba grumbled, and testily threw out a call at the men. "Come in— come in! What you waitin' on?"

Teke's horse came forward, Tarlton following, their horses' shoes making a clatter on the shale. Scrubby oak made a black mass behind them, moonlight throwing their shadows across the grass. Into the murk of the trees they pulled up, Tarlton swinging from his saddle stiffly. "Hear about Endite?"

"What about him?"

"Dead," the brand inspector said. "It's all over town. Somebody—mighta been that girl he had up there, polished him off with a Walker Colt."

"With a Walker, eh?" Calder murmured. "Still packin' yours, Tarlton?"

"Yeah. Coroner'll sit on the body at ten, case anybody's interested. Then they'll pack Frank over to the furniture—"

"Who the hell cares?" Teke snarled impatiently.

Tarlton said, "I was thinkin' Slank, here, might be wanting to see how a dead fool looks."

Rubelcaba laughed. "What's that girl say about it?"

"You got me." Tarlton rubbed at his nose. "Ain't heard she's made any comment; matter of fact, nobody knows where she is. She's skipped."

"Where the hell could she go?"

Impatiently Teke said to Rubelcaba, "When you're ready to put the skids under

Fiersen, I've got some info you might want
to use."

"How's that?"

"If I was wanting to make him riled,"
Teke said, "I'd figure some way to get hold
of that kid."

Calder's horse in the shadows danced two
quick steps. Teke's breath hung up and
cold steel scraped from Rubelcaba's armpit.
"Pull up, you rannies! I'll say who's to be
shot—an' when! Quit wranglin' and listen.
Here's how we'll work this . . ."

TWENTY-TWO

TAISY HAD NO means of guessing how long
she'd remained in that world of unfathomable blackness, but when she opened her
eyes it was to a sense of dim grayness she
was sure was a dream. She felt positive of
this because life wasn't like that. Life was a
noisome and awful thing filled with scurri-
lous laughter, humiliation, pain and heart-
ache. Of wriggling snakes and great black
caterpillars crawling and creeping among the
shadows. Life was a blinding light in your
eyes. Only dreams were filled with nice furniture. Only dreams had dear little curtains

with tufts of gay colors sewn onto them. Only dreams had shades at the windows and great wide beds with clean covers on them.

Taisy closed her eyes.

When she opened them again there was light in the room, a soft golden light that was yellow as butter. This came from a shaded lamp on a table and, alongside the table, there was a chair with a girl in it. Taisy had no idea who this was. Brown haired, lushly built and tanned by much sun. She had green eyes that were direct and steady, and lips that gave her a reckless look, red and full and, just now, rather bitter.

Taisy started to speak but the girl shook her head. "Just rest. You've got to keep quiet. Sleep if you can."

Taisy wondered about that, but didn't really care. She closed her eyes and when again she opened them it was broad daylight. The shades were raised and morning's sun lay bright on the bed, filling the room with its cheerful glow.

Taisy yawned and stretched. Even felt a little guilty when she thought of Mr. Gooms. Probably downstairs having a pretty purple fit because she was late getting up again.

He—"Lordy, lordy!" Taisy gasped, going completely pale as she recollected the snake and those desolate shadows. This wasn't her room at the Hairpin House. Lordy, where was she?

Then it came back in a rush of fragments. Frank's death, and her setting out to avenge him. Getting herself lost, the subsequent trouble with that horse she'd gone off on, the fall in the brush, that dratted rattler and the horrible knowledge of knowing herself doomed. After that for a bit the pictures got fuzzy; then she remembered this room and the girl in the chair.

Where had that green-eyed girl got to now? Was it her that was making those kitchen sounds yonder? Someone was sure shaking up a breakfast and the smell of good coffee made her throw back the covers, thrusting feet toward the floor.

Which was when she discovered she had been undressed with nothing on now but a mighty thin shift. Rucked up by her movements, this was well above her knees. But unconscious of this immodest exposure, Taisy stared at the discolored place on her leg, at the crosscut wound now bisecting the fang marks; and she shuddered at remembrance of that terrible night.

Her leg still felt sore but was no longer swollen. She guessed she felt pretty normal except she was hungry.

It was a mark of her changed mental attitude that she could sit there awhile regarding the wound instead of making all haste to snatch down the shift as she self-consciously would have a few days ago; the thought of hiding her legs simply did not occur to her. This was no extension of her relationship with Frank, but more an indication of normal healthy growth. She wasn't thinking of legs, nor much of Frank either. Her thoughts were concerned with her present whereabouts and how she had come here.

Even when she heard the turn of the doorknob, saw the door opening, she was not reminded to cover herself. Curiously she was staring at the brown-haired girl with the reckless face. Strangely enough those sea-green eyes reminded her of Fiersen, though she could not imagine why this should be so. Other than because of their steady scrutiny, there was no similarity.

The girl asked, "Are you feeling able to be up?"

"How long have I been here—I mean in this place? And what place is it?"

"You arrived here on Monday. Today is Thursday. You can eat in the kitchen if you want to get dressed. You'll find a pitcher of water and a basin yonder. There'll be a towel and wash cloth in the top left drawer."

Taisy smiled, trying to win some degree of warmth from the girl who continued to regard her with an odd kind of wariness. "My name's Taisy—Taisy Aiken."

"I know. You'll find your breakfast on the stove. Don't dawdle. I've a lot of things to look after; most of my work has to be done here in the morning. You'll find your clothes over there in that chair."

Nodding, she stepped back, closed the door and was gone.

Taisy stared at the door's blank panels with a halfway frown, shrugged and, pulling the shift up over her head, dropped it on the bed and went across to the wash stand. The water was cold like it had come from a spring. She felt a heap better as she got into her clothes—Frank's clothes really, and thrust her feet into Frank Endite's boots. Getting into those duds left her somewhat light-headed but, opening the door, she found herself in a hall. Coffee smell drew her into the kitchen where the green-eyed girl was washing pans in the sink. She pumped some water on her hands, wiped the hands on a flour sack and, going to the stove, dished up Taisy's breakfast.

Taisy stood by the table. "I could of done that."

"I do what I'm told. Within limits," the girl said, and poured Taisy's coffee. "You'd better tuck into that."

Taisy peered at her, wonderingly. "I had a gun . . ."

The girl put the coffeepot back on the stove and stepped to the screen that framed the back door. "Jordie," she called, "you keep away from them horses!"

She went back to the stove and picked up the skillet. Dislike was plain in the glance she flicked Taisy. "I only work here. You got any complaints you better talk to the boss," and sloshed the skillet around in the sudsy water as plain indication she had said all she aimed to.

Taisy shrugged off her notions in the pleasure of eating. She couldn't think why this girl was so unfriendly; letting Taisy have her bed shouldn't have aroused such hostility. Maybe, Taisy thought, it was Frank's clothes that upset her, though why this should be was just one more of the mysteries about her. Who was she, anyway? Taisy'd looked for rings but had not seen any. Evidently the girl took care of this place; maybe she was riled at having to feed another mouth. Cooks were generally a pretty cantankerous lot.

Still wondering about her, Taisy sampled the coffee and munched at her toast. Green Eyes yelled through the door again. "Jordie, you come in here!"

Some man's voice called, "He's all right, Cherry. I'm keepin' an eye on him—"

"I want him to start getting cleaned up for dinner."

"Shucks, he looks clean enough; he'll be all right."

Swishing flies from the screen with a flick of her apron, Cherry snatched up the skillet and banged it back on the stove.

"Sounds like your Ma's on the warpath this morning, son." Then a childish voice suddenly screamed with delight. Bootsteps came prancing across the yard. The man's voice said, "Hang hold there, boy!" and boots came clattering up to the door. The child screamed. The man nickered and pawed at the step.

"You're spoilin' him rotten," the girl, Cherry, complained; and Taisy swung round as she heard the screen opened, saw the boy sliding down off a man's broad shoulders, and went completely still as she peered up into the smiling face of the man she had come here to kill.

In the sheriff's office at Tucson, Blankenstraw who stood for the law in this section threw out plumb short hands expressively. "Gents, I'm sorry. You've got my sympathy. If there was any way I could help . . . but there ain't. I'm plumb shocked by these things you've been mentionin'. But as sheriff of this here county my hands is tied. Rules an' regulations—"

"Damn the regulations!" Joe Moses snarled explosively. "You reckon we've rode all them miles just to be hamstrung by a bunch of regulations? You're packin' the tin—we've come to you fer help! Didn't you hear me say there've been three women killed—three women murdered an' a young girl raped an' you got the guts t' stand there an' argue!"

"Just a minute, Joe," Rubelcaba put in. "Don't do no good to get in a lather. Callin' names never swobbed out no rifles. There ain't a forwarder lookin' man in this country today than Dave Blankenstraw. If there's any way he can help . . ." He eyed the sheriff enquiringly.

Blankenstraw frowned portentously, walked around his spur scarred desk and carefully eased his bulk into the chair. "I'm sorry, boys. I know how you feel, but this office was never intended for a constabulary. I just ain't got enough help to go round. There's a new bill up before the legislature now; but until and if this bill goes through, my hands is tied. This is too big a county for one man to handle—"

"All right," Moses nodded. "Swear us in an' we'll take care of it. An' we won't ask one damn cent for doin' it."

Blankenstraw, staring, shook his head. "I can't do that! Man alive—"

"Why not?"

"You might's well ask me to stick a gun in my mouth! If I was to do that . . . Nope, I can't go handin' out stars to half the interested parties in a range feud."

Moses bridled. "This ain't no range feud!"

"It sure looks like one to me."

Amos Tabbs cried bitterly. "Who you workin' for—the county or Fiersen? Jest answer me that! The county or that damn rustler?"

"I can't mix this office—"

Moses' black shape leaned over the desk, banging it fiercely with a massive fist. "We're a-talkin'," he snarled, "about plain damn anarchy! Man ain't safe in his own house no more! Honest ranchers bein' bushwhacked all over—hung from their rafters, dumped into cesspools! Stock run off, stock slaughtered! Women raped! Night ridin' vandals— Hell! If that don't call for the law's intervention I'd like, by God, to know what will get you off your fat ass!"

Sweat was a shine on the sheriff's red face. He dragged a plump finger around the inside of his collar. "If it's bad as that . . ." He took a fresh breath. "You keep talkin' about Fiersen but where's your evidence?"

"Ever'body *knows* it's Fiersen! You think we're *blind?*"

"If you know so much then all you got to do is swear out a warrant an' I'll get right over there an' pick him up."

Rubelcaba said, "How much proof—"

"To swear out a warrant? You'll have to make specific charges. You say there've been killin's. You'll have to put names to the victims and the names of whoever saw the accused—"

Moses swore. "If we could rake up all

that we wouldn't have needed to call on you."

The sheriff sighed and smoothed down the vest across his vast belly. "From the bottom of my heart you folks have my sympathy, but if you've got no witnesses—"

"C'mon," Rubelcaba said, "we'll git no help here. All this fence straddler's interested in is votes. He's fixin' to set right here—"

"You got no call to say that!" Blankenstraw's face was livid with fury. "I'll tell you somethin' else. You go takin' the law into your—"

"Let's git outen this snake den," Joe Moses snarled. "A couple dozen ropes'll take care of our problems, an' when that's tended to I guess we'll know what—"

Rubelcaba, shoving him toward the door, said, "That's enough, Joe. Button your lip and let's git whackin'."

TWENTY-THREE

WHO CAN SAY what alchemy of spirit a mind undergoes when invaded by shock? The wild events of these past several days had confounded, bewildered all of Taisy's perceptions. Though she did not recognize these changes in herself, the impact of recent happenings had lifted her out of the concepts of childhood, forcing her to face the pervading realities of a life that could never be the same again.

No longer was she the ignorant urchin who, flustered and flushed, had met Endite's stare across the length of that clatterous table. Nor the one who'd found him bloodily dying, rocked in her arms while his gambler's soul slipped across the Divide. Tattered vestiges remained, tangled in past loyalties—of what she felt she owed Frank, of those frightening horizons briefly glimpsed through the confusions of her scrambled emotions. Badly upset she found the Jade Fiersen confronting her now greatly unlike that merciless varmint she had carried in her head while bent over Frank, bitterly swearing to avenge him. Someway this Fiersen wasn't at all like she'd imagined.

In this startled moment, he seemed almost human; and yet *"Fiersen—"* Frank had whispered with his last gasping breath. However reluctant was this recollection, it was not a thing to be shoved to one side. Filled with conflicting needs, with strange yearnings, astonished and trembling she stared, mouth twisted with frustration.

Why couldn't he seem like that time in the Sparrowhawk when Mike Strawn's pistol had started all this? Cold and reckless, hard as granite, bleak as the windswept sand-riddled miles—that was how she wanted to be seeing him, red with Frank's blood, a cowardly thief pounding off through the night.

"How'd I git here?"

"Why, ma'am, I reckon me and Ginger fetched you from out in the brush, thrashin' around, talking mighty fierce-like. You was some put out with that snake . . . You'll be right enough now."

She pulled her eyes off him, looking past the black shape of him limned against the sun swept yard. This was the devil she had set out to kill and nothing was going to undermine that intention. Some snakes could look mighty handsome, too, but they could bite just as fierce as them ugly ones! He'd gunned Frank down without a chance—hadn't she seen him running for that Bar D horse?

She searched the highboned planes of his face. "That night," she said, "that night you found me . . . What color shirt did you have on?"

He looked surprised, but said easily enough, "A gray one, ma'am, if that makes any difference."

"What'd you do with that green one you had?"

"I expect it's round here someplace." Smiling, he said, "You partial to green?"

Why didn't the dratted polecat look guilty? Instead of like a feller trying to figure what she was getting at? But coyotes never looked guilty, either, and lying was part of his stock in trade. She'd better remember that. "What color horse was you ridin'?"

"Ginger's a sorrel."

"Could I have a look at him?"

"I reckon you could." He glanced at her slanchways. "What's this all about, ma'am?" The smile still was on him but it wasn't any longer lighting up his look.

"If you got nothin' to hide let me see him. Now."

Fiersen shrugged and winked at the child who was solemnly watching around the edge of his mother's skirt. Jordie tried to wink back and Fiersen slapped his thigh. "Well, come on," he sighed. "Ginger's out in the corral—reckon you can make it that far?"

She glared at him scornfully. Strangely enough it didn't occur to her to be frightened. She looked at the boy and held out her hand. "You want to go, Jordie?"

The boy's eyes brightened up.

The boy's mother said curtly, "He's got to have his bath."

Jordie's grin tumbled off. "Oh, let the boy go, Cherry. Won't be but a couple of minutes," Fiersen said. "I'll keep close watch of him."

Cherry wheeled away with a flounce of skirts. Taisy, having caught the glint of her look, hesitantly said, "If it can wait till we get back, I'd be real glad to—" and let the rest fall away, startled by the anger in the other woman's face.

Fiersen glanced from one to the other, let his breath out softly and, picking up Jordie, sat the boy on his shoulder. He turned out through the screen and Taisy hurried after them. She called, "Let's see if Jordie can pick out Ginger."

Fiersen glanced at her curiously, stood frowning a moment. With a short kind of nod, he struck off toward the corral.

There were seven or eight horses in the

pen he went up to, a man idly lounged against the peeled pole bars. He had on a blue shirt and a pair of scuffed chaps, and the seat of his pants held the shine of much riding. He slewed a swift look at the sound of their approach and Fiersen told Taisy, "My range boss, Michael Strawn," and the man jerked his head.

He was exactly as Taisy remembered him, incredibly redheaded with brick-bronze skin and a blue kind of stare that was cynical and doubting, like the night he'd shot Endite on the turn of a card. A discontented brashness shaped all his features and he remembered her at once. "This the one that got snake bit?"

Fiersen nodded; and Strawn said, "I'll take the snake," and grinned at her wickedly.

Fiersen stopped in his tracks, stopped so short Jordie grabbed at him. The screen door banged and Cherry Grant strode toward them. Fiersen's look considered Strawn. "What was that?"

"By God!" ground out Strawn. "Can't you see it?" An acid bitterness burned through his words. "Why don't you wake up to what's goin' on in this patch of catclaw? Wonder to me you ain't been planted a'ready!" Contempt put a mean look into his stare. "Said you found this girl in the brush out yonder—what in God's name d'you reckon she was doin' there?"

"I haven't asked," Fiersen said.

Strawn snorted.

Cherry Grant came up but nobody looked at her. Jordie, one chubby fist gripping Fiersen, pointed with the other at the bunched-up horses. "Genger!" he squealed. "Genger, Mama!"

Taisy, caught by locked stares, hardly noticed the horse; it wasn't the one Frank's killer had mounted. Was it Strawn who had killed Frank? Frank had said "Fiersen—" and she wanted to believe it, having in mind that night at the Sparrowhawk and what Tabbs had told her of homesteaders driven from their land at gunpoint, ranches raided in the pale gloom of dawn. And, suddenly, it was all too much for her. "You gunman!" she cried. "You drygulchin' killer!" and tried to get her hands on his pistol; but Strawn, reaching out, threw her off balance. Jordie howled in alarm and, with a fierce look at Taisy, his mother grabbed him and swept him off toward the house.

"Reckon that's plain enough," Strawn told

Fiersen. "Even you should be bright enough to latch onto that."

Fiersen paid him no notice. Eyeing Taisy, he said, "That's the second time you've called me a killer. I'm asking you why?"

"Gawd!" Strawn swore. "Didn't you see her in the bar bawlin' over that tinhorn? Endite's dead an' she figures you killed him."

In the following silence, a wind off the foothills washed up the sound of an approaching horse. Nobody gave it any attention. Fiersen's face showed surprise, frowningly shaded by something less readable. "Go on," Strawn growled. "Whyn't you ask her. I don't guess she'd bother lyin' about it."

As though to something in his mind, Fiersen's head tipped. "That why you asked what shirt I was wearin'? What horse I was ridin'?"

Taisy, striving to keep herself hardened against him, nodded.

"Then I expect you must have got a look at the killer. You rightdown sure he was wearin' my shirt?"

He could tell by the angry look of her she was. "But you never saw his face?"

She saw what he was getting at and

thought this about the outside of enough. "I saw him get onto a Bar D horse!" she eyed him fiercely. "I didn't have to see your face! You had on that same green shirt I saw you wearin' that night at the Sparrowhawk! An' when you lit out I could see you was headin' straight for this ranch!"

"That settles it!" Strawn snarled. "I been tellin' you fer months there was crooks on this payroll! Some varmint put on your shirt, rode a Bar D horse an' went into Dry Bottom an' killed that gambler—now ask me why!"

"I'm asking you," Fiersen said, and suddenly turned still.

They all heard it then, the wind rushing sound from an oncoming pony. Coming like blue blazes; and they saw the rider break from the trees. It was Calder, the Bar D foreman, a wild high shape on the foam flecked pony. "Brand blotted cattle—" his voice was a shout. "At Huerfano Butte! Brand blotted Spanish Cross critters!"

TWENTY-FOUR

Strawn said, "Christ!" and broke for his rope.

When he came high-heeling back with it, bound for the pen and shaking out a loop, Fiersen called, "Wait a minute."

Calder came down off his horse on the run but at Fiersen's words he braked to a stop. Like Strawn, he sent a quick searching look at the face of this man who paid their wages. Strawn snarled, awash with impatience.

"We're not going off half cocked," Fiersen told them.

"Not goin'!" Strawn cried, harsh in the grip of a stark amazement. "You figure to leave them cattle there? Don't you savvy it's a *trap?*"

"Which is why we're not rushing into it," Jade answered. "And if it's just a red herrin', we got no time for it." He said to Calder, "How many cattle?"

"I dunno—plenty! They was scattered all over that ridge to the south."

"Any riders?"

Calder shook his head. "If it's figured to look like we stole them, wouldn't be much point sendin' out no crew."

"Where's our outfit?" Fiersen slammed at Strawn.

The range boss pitched down his rope

with a curse. "Don't ask *me*—I only work here!"

"I've got the boys," Calder said, "out in them canyons west of the Haystack Peaks."

"Better send Lumpy—"

"We goin' after Rubelcaba?" Strawn growled, showing interest.

"No," Fiersen answered.

"Expect we better leave the crew where they're at. Lot of our beef's got into those canyons," Calder remarked.

"Rubelcaba," Fiersen said, "ain't much interested in our stuff at the moment," and Mike Strawn looked uncharitably at him, eyes darkly mirroring the thoughts in his head.

But Fiersen knew Strawn clean down to his bootheels, understood all too well the way of Strawn's notions. All old ties between them were severed, worn away that night Jade had brought out the doc to fetch Cherry's young one. Strawn thought Fiersen to be the father of the child and only one thing still held Strawn here, an unchanging loyalty to the memory of Jade's father who had found young Mike hiding out in the brush near the smoldering ruins of an ambushed wagon train. But the time was nearing when the last lean doubt would drop out of his mind. When that time came, Strawn would turn on Fiersen like a rabid wolf.

Nevertheless Fiersen said, "What's eatin' you, Mike?"

"By Gawd, if you're afraid of that bastard you better be hittin' a lope for the tules!"

"I been thinkin' about it," Fiersen smiled; and Taisy chose that moment to cry at him sharply: "I want my gun!"

Without remark, Fiersen got Frank's derringer from his pocket and gave it into her hand. Plainly this astonished her, and he watched contradictory emotions pass through her stare, watched her suddenly point the pistol at him desperately and his eyes widened some but it did not seem to scare him.

"Rubelcaba's claimin' round town," mentioned Calder, "that we've run off Yates an' Blakely, that it's us wrecked Turkey Track an' them other outfits; that he could easy name who raped that girl an' killed them other three to shut their mouths—same snake, he says, that's got one kid out at Bar D now from a unwed mother."

And stepping back a pace, he watched Mike Strawn.

The man's gleaming stare was almost black. There was sweat on his face, but all it got out of him was "Reckon that's all we'll be needin' to know. Which horse you takin'?"

Fiersen blew out a breath and shook his head.

"Well, damn my soul!" Strawn shouted and stood with hot unbelieving eyes. Then his mouth clamped shut with a snap of teeth and he grabbed up his rope and ducked through the pen's rails.

"Where now?" Fiersen called.

"Don't figure I'm fixed to stay here no more." All the fury of months poured out of him then. "This spread used to know how to take care of— Hell! there used to be some pride in this outfit till you come back an' started walkin' on eggshells. You slink through the brush like a damn coyote!"

"Careful, Mike," Fiersen said, turning pale.

Strawn sneered. "That's all a man hears outa you anymore—careful! Is it the sun makes you look so goddam yeller?"

"You better go," Fiersen said, his features tightening up like something chopped out of wood. Taisy stared at him, scarce breathing. But he said nothing more. Calder stood by his horse, enigmatically watching and, someway, Taisy felt like crying.

Strawn roped out a horse, piled on his saddle, led the animal out and put up the bars; and all this while Fiersen stood there, silent. Strawn rode off and Fiersen stayed where he was, staring down at his hands. He seemed old-man tired, chin sunk almost onto his chest. With a gust of breath, he brought up his head and Taisy couldn't help feeling how friendless and lost was the dreary look of this man she had taunted, called gunman and killer. His cheeks turned darker when he saw her watching, but still he did not break into speech, nor did he appear to be condemning Strawn, as she was.

Taisy caught her breath, turning that over. *What kind of person was she, taking up for the back-shooting varmint that had downed Frank Endite!*

Her cheeks burnt with shame. Frank deserved better.

She glared at Fiersen—why did she find it so hard to hate him? How could he so damnably excite her sympathy? Was it because everybody seemed so hardset against him? She said with her hauled up glance bright with malice: "Looks like your birds is comin' home to roost."

"Yes," he nodded. "I've been expectin' them to." No reproach, no bitterness, no anger in him. She'd been sure his glance would turn wild and ugly. She wanted him to look the killer he was.

Calder stirred by his horse. Taisy stabbed her eyes at him, saw his twisted grin. She remembered the weight of Frank in her arms and lifted the derringer until it was pointed square at Jade's heart.

TWENTY-FIVE

FURIOUS SHE SAID, "Throw up your hands!"

She'd been half scared she couldn't nerve herself up to shooting him and was glad to find her hand wasn't shaking, the steel of the trigger coolly firm against her finger. He deserved to die and she was going to kill him.

She realized then he was coming toward her, slowly, catlike, holding her with that glittery stare. He was smiling and she suddenly knew she never could do it.

She flung down Frank's gun with a smothered cry, bitterly sobbing behind hands thrown up to hide her tears. Through the blur of fingers, she could see him still, scarred face sober, a dark unreadable frown etched across it and, abruptly, he was reaching out for her. Now she was against him, shaking, still sobbing; and she buried her face against his shoulder, shutting out the sight of Calder's cynical grin.

Then the foreman went off with his horse toward the barn and she heard Jade softly talking and talking and she cried all the harder for—though her cheeks were hot from the knowledge of it—she liked mighty well to be where she was with Fiersen's arm clamped that way around her. She shut her eyes tight the better to savor its goodness and found herself wondering if this were love.

It was brazen to think of love and Jade Fiersen; and worse when she remembered poor Frank a-dying. She hated herself for this seemed like betrayal and she shoved Fiersen back, straining against that encircling arm, striving to break that hold and get loose of him.

But he plain wouldn't let her. When she tipped back her head to lash out at him, he pulled her even more tightly against him, crushing her mouth with his hungry lips. Time stopped completely. Her soaring spirit hit the rim of the world and she tore out of his clutch like a clawing wildcat.

"Damn you!" she panted. "Damn you,

Jade Fiersen!" and crouched there quivering like a wounded doe. A thunder like surf roared and crashed at her ears. The yard was an uptilted flash of flame; earth, sky and trees whirled dizzily round her.

The feel of his lips was like a brand searing into her, marking her his for all time to come. "I hate you!" she cried, spat out his kiss, scrubbing a hand across her mouth. "If there's a God lookin' down at us, you'll pay for this!"

And she could see him now, standing perfectly still. He opened his face and closed it again and she could hear the awful pound of her heart. He came against her again and she hung there stiff as a sun cured hide, wanting him and hating him both at once.

He let go of her then and stepped back, arm half lifted, stopped by what he thought was her fury, her eyes like the look of a chain-held lynx—he could think of no other way to describe her. This outraged look of her moved him deeply. He kept watching her, silent and thoroughly disturbed.

"I'll not claim I'm sorry, Taisy. It ain't in me to be sorry for the joy that gave me—I won't ask you to forgive me for I see you can't. But I want you to know I meant every bit of it."

His big shoulders arched and he shrugged impatiently. "I reckon love comes to folks in damn strange ways—"

"Love!" Taisy cried, and shuddered, glaring.

"I know," Fiersen said. "Guess I can't blame you; I been wantin' to do that a right long while, ever since in fact I saw you at Slocum's. You called me a thief an' I expect, deep down, that described me plumb certain. I'd have taken you away from that gambler then if I'd seen any way I could do it."

He paused, morosely considering her, then said abruptly, "I'll not hold you against your will. If you're bent on leavin', I'll not try to stop you."

Her stormy, hating eyes raked across him, but he could not know it was herself she hated. He could not make her out at all. She looked so alone, so frail and forlorn, it churned up the misery inside him. This tragic look of her tore at his heart, and he cursed himself for the haste that had lost her, that had spoilt all chance of his suit succeeding before she'd had any real chance to know him. In her mind, he reckoned, he was naught but a bullying gunman—and worse.

Well, he'd thrown his chance away on an impulse—just like he'd done back at Six-Shooter Siding when he'd thrown his gun on that damned Sam Ketchum and dropped instead an honest marshal.

He'd no way of guessing it was her own treacherous heart which had roused Taisy's fury, that she'd wanted him to do just what he'd done; that, after the manner of women since Eve, she had brought about the situation; that her own flushed cheeks and trembling body—something glimpsed in her stare, were as much to be blamed as his loss of control.

"Better pick up that gun," he told her gruffly. "There's damned lonesome country between here an' town."

Just minutes ago, she'd have jumped at any chance to get clear; now wild horses couldn't have dragged her away. She had no intention of leaving Bar D until what was between them was resolved. She'd got to deal this yellow-haired devil every bit of the anguish inside her if she was ever to forget her own black treachery and grant Frank a chance to rest quiet in his grave.

Fiersen himself had shown her how she might do this though she believed it was God had shown her the way. She would use this brazen love he professed—yes, and make out of it the rope he'd be hoist on. She'd then have done her duty by Frank and could forget the wicked wanting of her heart.

"I'll stay on a while," she said, picking up poor Frank's dropped gun, and shook and thumped it to clear the barrel before she dropped it into a pocket. Flashing Jade Fiersen a scornful glance, she passed him with a swinging step and headed for the house. If she could not kill that devil herself, she could at least hang and rattle until somebody else did. When the valley ranchers stormed this place, she would find some way to bring him into their hands.

Dinner still wasn't ready when she stepped inside and she could find no wish for Cherry Grant's sour company. She was traversing the hall to reach her room when "Oh, Miz Aiken," the green-eyed girl called, "don't you think little Jordie takes after his Paw?"

Taisy's ears felt hot and she marched right along; she couldn't have faced Cherry then for anything. Stumbling, she entered her room and slammed the door, but couldn't shut out the girl's mocking laugh.

She'd forgotten little Jordie when Fiersen kissed her—forgotten Frank, too! But now, thinking back to Fiersen's arm round her, she guessed she'd been just about ready, right on the edge of throwing up everything. She realized now she purely couldn't. Jordie *did* look like him! In an odd kind of way. At least he had the same eyes, even some of Jade's gestures. Half the valley believed Jordie was Jade Fiersen's kid. Even Mike Strawn, who sure hadn't wanted to, obviously believed—it was this conviction which had driven him away.

She hadn't realized that before. Why had she come here? Why had she ever got into this mess! Why couldn't she have let the valley take care of him? She always seemed to be doing the wrong thing; ever since she'd borrowed that dress to meet Frank, she'd had nothing but trouble. She reckoned God was paying her back for her sins.

A long while later, someone knocked on the door. She guessed it was Fiersen by the heavy sound of him—by the way her heart jumped; but she wouldn't answer.

When he left, she flung open the door and ran after him, caught sight of the back of him going into the office. Without pausing to consider, she went in there, too; pushed the door to and leaned against it, heart thudding.

It was that hard green sheen of his eyes, she guessed, that made the strike of his glance so disconcerting. The long solid lips locked together. There was a quick streak of pressure along Fiersen's jaws as though, about to say something, he had changed his mind; then it burst from him anyway. "You're powerful easy on the eyes!"

Taisy flushed, but she couldn't help feeling set up by his words. You could tell pretty words didn't come easy to him. You could tell he meant it! The throaty sound of his voice drove Frank and everything else from her mind; there was just the two of them, staring at each other.

It made her catch her breath. "Lordy, Jade! The way you're a-lookin' at me!"

She marveled she wasn't afraid of him. Some men a girl had to watch every minute; it just wasn't that way with Fiersen. Despite all the talk—everything she'd heard of him— she could tell Jade Fiersen wasn't that kind of gent.

"You know," he said, "I wish you'd tell me about Frank's death." He considered his rope-scarred hands, eyed her somberly. "I ain't wanting to be hurtin' you, Taisy, but it might help if I knew what you remember about it."

Perfectly still, her look oddly intent—searching, actually, all the angles of her face became shadowed with thinking, hands gripped tightly.

"It wasn't me killed Frank," Fiersen told her. "I would like mighty well to find out who did. I reckon if I could get my hands on that jasper—"

"Hands!" Taisy cried, going still as death. Oh, how she wished he never had said it for it called up a picture better forgotten—eight grubby fingers clamped to the window ledge of Frank's room.

She shut her eyes but continued to see them. Then, quick as a flash she snatched out Frank's derringer. "Grab a-holt of the top of that desk!"

Fiersen's lips came apart in a short gruff laugh.

"Grab a-holt!" Taisy breathed, thinly close to hysteria.

With eyes going narrowly dark, Fiersen did so.

Taisy stared at the fingers, cheeks turning suddenly white as bone. The hand holding Frank's gun fell against her leg. "Oh, Jade—" she cried, and would surely have fallen had he not caught her. She trembled against him, clutching him tightly, and looked up into his face with such fright he laughed a little, sort of husky and shaken. "What is it, Taisy?"

"Lordy, lordy!" came an anguished whisper. "Good lordy, Jade—I—I come mighty close to shootin' the wrong man!"

She told him all she could recall. Cheeks flushed, words tumbling excitedly over each other, she told of seeing the killer's fingers clamped to the outside ledge of Frank's window. "I can see them plain as I can see you—hard an' tight they was pressed to that sill, dirt in the nails an' one of them bleedin' where the nail was broke down into the quick—so it couldn't of been you . . . Oh, Jade, I'm so glad!"

"I'm pretty glad myself. Frank must have known too much about somebody." He squeezed her shoulder. "Think, Taisy—try and think back to whatever Frank said. There must have been *some*thing."

She stared at him, trying to fetch back that terrible moment. "He was tryin', I think, to tell me something but alls he said was '*Fiersen*—' like that. Then I saw them fingers. The feller let go an' I saw him, dressed like you, a-streakin' for that Bar D horse, an' I plain up an' reckoned Frank was meanin' you killed him."

"I expect he might have thought it was me," Fiersen mused, scowling. "You ever see Frank talking with anyone—I mean like maybe he didn't want to be seen or heard?"

"After he got shot in that saloon, he never did have no chance to do that." She shook her head from side to side. "I'm pretty sure now he was tryin' to—*maybe* it was somethin' I was to tell *you*. He called out your name. He grabbed at his side and fell down on the floor an' never spoke another word." She scrinched up her eyes. "He mighta been wantin' somethin' out of his pocket. When I looked there was a folded-up paper there. Pretty much blurred from packin' it around, but there was just the two words . . . The last word was Carver. It had a capital C."

Of a sudden, Fiersen's face looked strangely tight. She could feel that tension creeping all through him, and she stared at him, scared, and shook his arm. "Does it help?"

He drew a gusty breath, let it drearily go. "I can see now what a durn fool I have been," and she could feel the muscles bunch in his arm. She felt raw temper in the grip

261

of his fingers. Without mentioning names, he told her about being in Tucumcari with Ketchum. "While we were in that place, two men came in, one of them a marshal; someone had told him where to find the man who was with me. The second of this pair was the no-good brother of the man I was with. Behind the other, we didn't look at him proper—our eyes, I guess, was too full of that marshal. We'd dragged our irons quick as we saw him, was hopin' to get out of there without no fuss.

"We were backing away, trying to get to a window, when somebody prodded up hell with a pistol. It was that sidewinder hid out behind the marshal. I was hit—I could feel that slug like a hunk of fire. I snapped off a shot but it was the marshal that staggered. He jerked clear back and fell into a table. My partner had just got out through the window. Half blinded, crazy with pain, I jumped after him. They were all shooting now but we got away."

He stepped back a pace. When she did not speak, he drew a long breath. "I've never forgotten that business, don't expect I ever will. It brought me back here; perhaps it's led me to play into the hands . . . I'm the 'Bill Carver' Frank wrote on that paper.

Had a hunch I'd seen him someplace before. We was buckin' Frank's game when Sam fetched that marshal. Six-Shooter Siding was what they called the place then."

He took a quick turn up and down the room, battling himself, restlessness driving him, heckled by things churned out of the past. He came wheeling back to her.

In a harsh grinding voice he said, "I'm not going to be very good for you, Taisy. Mine is the blame for what happened to that lawman—for what's been goin' on here, like enough, besides. I should of stopped this—could have; I just didn't want no more of this gun stuff—was hoping to stay out of it. The folks who've been killed would be alive right now had I done what I could—if I'd stopped Rubelcaba when I first guessed what he had in his mind. Rubelcaba told me a long time ago *'Ten years from now I'm goin' to own this country'*—that's what he's up to, tryin' to make that brag good."

"Why are you a-tellin' me this?"

"Because I love you, Taisy. Because I want you more than anything on earth; you're the only woman I've said that to— the only one I ever *will* say it to; but I've found you too late. Even if you could bring yourself to believe me, even if you could

263

learn to care, it just ain't in the cards we could make something of it. What's happening here is bigger than we are—bigger than any two people in the world. The fate of this valley an' every critter in it is dependin' on somebody stoppin' Rubelcaba. I'm allowin' that chore belongs to me."

"But—" She put a hand on his arm.

"You don't see it, girl! I thank God you don't; but there's just one way I can do it, and doin' it that way won't bring us together."

Some of what he'd said she couldn't understand and she plain didn't notice that last remark. She was too busy tracing out a notion of her own, facing the room's one open window, watching the shadows lengthen out in the yard, watching the gloom building up where the bunch grass thinned underneath the trees. She knew a vague surprise at the swiftness with which this day had passed, and wondered why Cherry hadn't called them to eat, why the Bar D crew had not put in an appearance. All these were gnawing at the back of her mind. In the front of her thoughts was a buoyant euphoria, the lift of her spirits now that she knew Fiersen had not killed Frank.

She wished she knew what Frank had

been trying to say to her. She thought abruptly to see something move out there, like the shape of a head wheel across the ground; but when she scrinched up her eyes the only shadows to be seen were those made by the trees. Some leafy branch, she guessed, tossed by the wind, and failed to notice that no wind was blowing.

"There was a letter there, besides, in Frank's pocket I mean—no address on it an' sealed up tight. I hid it in his room. Maybe we ought to get it."

She guessed he didn't hear, judging by the way he stood staring at nothing like his thoughts were a couple of million miles away. Reaching out she timidly touched him, like she was afraid he'd maybe go up in a puff of smoke; and said on a sudden rush of feeling: "I'm sure hangin' firm to what you told me. I wish it was in me to be a-bringin' you more. I been a terrible woman. I—I've done things would make you shake to think on. I come here to kill you—just like Strawn said. I can see now how it were the devil a-workin' in me, but I purely thought it was poor Frank's blood a-callin' on the Lord fer me to revenge him."

She peered at him anxiously. "When I seen you, though, then I knowed fer sure I couldn't never do it. When I seen you a-standin' there lookin' at me, that was when I first knowed what lovin' might be like. I'd go with you anywheres you'd be a-wantin' only . . . Jade, don't be leavin' me."

He looked down into her face and sighed, put his hands on her shoulders and pulled her to him, and they stood that way a long time without speaking. The smell of her hair was sweet in his nostrils and the heavy bunched muscles along his jaws tightened and clamped teeth choked back a sound of despair.

He was seeing that Tucumcari marshal falling through the whorls of powdersmoke and he knew in his bones there could be no escape. Even should he survive what he meant to do now, there would still be the business of that shot-down lawman. Gallows bait, he reckoned, was the right name for him. But he would do what he had to.

He should never have said he loved her; he could have spared her that, and should have. When he found her looking up at him, he strove to shake the gray gloom off his cheeks. "Jade," she said, "I got a hunch we ought to go after that letter—"

Fiersen shook his head.

"You don't reckon Frank wrote it?"

266

"If he did, I don't guess he wrote it for me. Someone else likely wrote it and passed it to Frank to hold onto for him."

"You figure it's somethin' could be used against you? Somethin' about that marshal, maybe?"

"I don't expect it would help much."

"Then we better git a-holt of it," Taisy cried.

He wanted to say nothing was like to help him but could not kill her last hope in that fashion. She was bound and determined to see him saved; if the note proved dangerous she meant to destroy it; but he knew too well he'd reached the end of his rope. When a man grabs a gun, he's gambling with death. And this was the only way to stop Rubelcaba, and he could not think he'd get loose of the man alive.

Better to encourage her, better to suggest she ride in and fetch it; that way, at least, she'd be away from any fracas. He was opening his mouth to put this to her when the stiff, fixed look of her struck him silent. She was peering through the open top half of the window.

With a grunt, he sprang past her and looked for himself. He'd a gun in his fist but there was nothing to shoot at, just the slap of a skirt going around the far corner.

He pulled in his head and took a sharp look at Taisy. Her glance met his, dark and round and frightened. "Cherry?" she said.

Fiersen stared out the window. "Expect you'd better take off for town. That letter . . ." Yes, that was it, play up the letter and get her away from here. He thrust some money into her hand. "Get a room at the hotel and stay there till you hear from me." He must give her no chance to argue. "I'll go saddle a bronc."

He started for the door. The sound of hoofs pounded off to the south. Taisy said from the window, "It's her—her an' Calder! An' Jordie!"

Fiersen said almost under his breath, "Just as well, I reckon," but did not tell her he had long suspected Bar D's foreman. Nor did he say that only little Jordie's smiling face had kept him from demanding an accounting of Calder. A child can't pick its father, has to make the best of the one he gets.

Jade turned through the kitchen, stopped by the kak-pole and got his rope and guessed while at it he'd saddle one for himself.

A good idea but late in arriving.

The sound of shod hoofs beat against the buildings. Fiersen cursed and whirled. He was a bounding shape, doubled over, diving doorward when Spanish Cross boiled through the trees with guns blazing.

TWENTY-SIX

Splinters jumped from the kitchen doorframe. A dishpan wailed off the wall beside it, throwing out a clatter of sound as it fell. A slug hammered through the slack of his vest and the glint of his eyes turned nearly black when he caught the dying screams of penned horses. He fell and lurched upright again. And then he was inside, dropping the bar on the slammed-shut door while lead carried all of the glass from the window and battered the walls like track layers' sledges.

From the flat of his belly, he came onto one knee, catching up the rifle from where it stood beside the door, and grinned when a man abruptly pitched from the saddle, when another wildly grabbed for the horn. The yard was a turmoil of dust and shadows as low crouched riders fanned into the trees.

He caught up a cartridge box, up-ending

it into one of his pockets, fed fresh shells into the heat of the magazine. There were seven or eight guns driving lead at the building and he could hear the Spanish Cross foreman's voice damning his crew for letting Fiersen reach cover.

He risked another quick look along the edge of the window. Bullets knocked chips from the frame and he ducked. But he'd seen enough. That bunch out there was re-shaping again under the lash of the foreman's blistering.

Fiersen called to Taisy: "Keep down on the floor where their lead can't touch you."

An upslamming shout sailed out of the trees. "Get in there now—get in there an' git him!" and both of them heard the hard rush of horses, and Fiersen lifted his weight again and had his quick glimpse of dust wreathed bodies slogging it toward him across the bare yard.

Contemptuous of whining lead, he grimly picked his targets and fired, watching that blast break them up and turn them, pitching them into colliding confusion. One gurgling yell fled into the trees. A man dead ahead flung out both arms and went backwards over the croup of his horse. Now they were scattering.

Fiersen dropped below the sill and sweat-
ily thrust fresh loads in his weapon. Next
time he looked, a pair of crouched rannies
were fading into the barn; and there wasn't
much need to guess what they were up to—
they were toting a five gallon can between
them. He lifted the rifle. Flame stabbed
twice from its swung-level barrel and one of
the two jerked forward and dropped; the
other one made it inside with the can.

Jade's thousand dollar stallion was in that
barn. He ground his teeth in impotent fury.

It began to look like this would be his last
stand and he tried to think how to get Taisy
out of it. No point saying they didn't know
she was here; they must suppose Cherry
Grant was around someplace. They weren't
about to let that interfere with their intentions.

Something then pulled his glance toward
the hall and there was Taisy, crouched in
the doorway with Frank's little gun grimly
gripped in her hand. She loosed a wan smile.
There was fright in the drawn, pinched lines
of her face and by that smile he knew the
depth of her courage.

It swayed him like a heavy wind. If there
were only some way he might get her out
. . . A lump came up and stuck in his throat

271

for the wistful way she was now looking at him. He smothered a groan, irritably swearing, cursing the folly that had gotten them trapped here; he'd always known that sooner or later . . . A muscle began to cramp in his shoulder and he scrubbed a hand across smarting eyes.

Out yonder, the night was but a whisper away. The sun was gone behind the western peaks and the glow had been leached from the cloud banks there, turning them the color of dirty wool. The continuing desultory *spat-spat* of rifles made wicked little tongues of flame across the gloom that was shrouding those cottonwoods yonder. The raid was deteriorating into a siege.

On hands and knees, Fiersen crawled to the hall and Taisy came sighingly into his arms and he held her close, feeling the rasp of his beard on her cheek, smelling the clean fresh scent of her hair. All the long hungers reawakened in him and all his thinking went racketing down a black shaft of despair.

"Taisy—" he said in a choked-tight voice, and she laid soft fingers over his mouth. "Just hold me." She let the hand fall away and he kissed her hopelessly; and with her arms crept around his neck they crouched, listening to the Spanish Cross rifles and the strike of bullets against adobe walls.

A glow presently stole through the kitchen windows and redly licked at their hands and faces. Fiersen jumped up with a sultry curse to see sparks swirling above the barn and flames breaking yellow through smoke along the roof. Thought of his stallion almost unnerved him.

Pain squeezed against the green glare of his eyeballs, their lids felt graveled with unshed tears. His fists hung knotted, despair clawed the look of him. He'd have gone out then but could see no use in it. Fiersen, with them, was but a side issue. It was the valley they were after . . .

Jade stiffened in his tracks. "By God!" he said with heart jammed hard against his ribs.

Were those fellows out there really *trying* to kill him? Thinking back of a sudden he was a little surprised. In Rubelcaba's boots this wasn't how he'd have run things . . . not if the object was Fiersen's death. They could have cut him down without loss of a man. They could have let him go into that corral and then shot him, could have dropped him easy from those trees with a rifle. Why hadn't they?

He could see it now. A dead scapegoat was no good to Rubelcaba. They wanted him alive, hid out in the hills where he couldn't be kept track of, where he could not interfere with the planned finale. Yes, that was it! They wanted him rushing around through the hills, knowing he'd keep until they'd got at the rest of it. Till they'd got all the other fools whipped into line.

"Fiersen! Talk up!"

"Well?" Fiersen said.

"Any females in there?"

When Jade didn't answer, Rubelcaba's foreman said, "Better git 'em out. How many's there?"

"Just one," Fiersen told him above Taisy's protests.

"Okay—send her out an' be quick about it. One of the boys'll catch up a bronc for her."

"She's wearing pants. Don't turn your guns on her." He caught Taisy's shoulders. "You've got to do this—"

"Please, Jade—no! Don't make me leave you."

"It's our best chance. Believe me. You get on that horse and hit for town. Don't lose any time—I'll get out of this; they're not here to kill me—back of this place has been left wide open. They're wantin' to have me shoved off in those gulleys."

"But they'll burn—"

"Never mind. If I can get into town, I can maybe get a handle on . . . Get going, Taisy!"

"But—Jade, I'm afraid!"

The Spanish Cross foreman bellowed impatiently. "If that girl's comin' out—"

"She's coming," Fiersen said. "Damn door's wedged; she'll have to come through the window."

"Well, hurry it up!"

Fiersen could not like any part of this except—if one could trust them—this could get her safely away. She was not safe here. "Remember. Go," he whispered, "straight for the Hairpin House; that's where I'll look for you." He gave her shoulder a shove toward the window. "She's comin'," he called, and watched her crawl through. Then he yanked off his boots and ran down the hall and into a room on the house's far side; pulled his boots on and got out through a north-facing exit, waiting, crouched over, until he heard Rubelcaba's man yell, "Hurry it up!" and a rattle of hoofs setting off toward the town.

He waited no longer, moving into the

trees where shadows concealed him, working through these in the direction of the barn's back side. He could hear his horse now in a frenzy of stamping, in terror of the smoke and heat from the flames. He knew any moment the fire might reach the hay in the loft, and when that happened . . .

Fiersen was about to break into a run when something heard stopped him short in his tracks. Searching the gloom, he dropped into a crouch, lifting his sixshooter out of its leather. Someone was moving around just ahead of him, somewhere between where Jade stood and the barn. The fellow moved again, a bent-over shape with a gun, tensely listening.

And now he was coming on again, cautiously, as though not sure where or what he was stalking. Fiersen hoped the man would blunder on by; the last thing wanted right now was attention.

Fiersen scarcely dared draw breath, but the fellow must have felt his presence. Not an arm's length away, he abruptly quit moving. Fiersen swung a gun weighted fist but it beat empty air as the man shied away. Jade sprang desperately as flame ripped a streak from a lifting pistol. He struck out again and this time the man dropped.

Already the flames from the burning barn were throwing their dancing light across the yard. Rubelcaba's crew were charging the house again and he could hear the foreman's voice shouting orders. "If he ain't in there, he can't have got far—set it afire an' start beatin' the bushes!"

Breaking into a run, Jade pulled open the barn's northside door, smoke belching into his face, almost blinding him. Flinging an arm up before his eyes, he shoved on through, hearing the terrified squeals of his stallion beating the box stall apart with shod hoofs, trying to get loose from the halter rope holding him.

A soft whinny went up somewhere off to the right and Jade recalled with dismay there'd been another in here, a bred mare. He spun that way with a bitter oath. She whinnied again as he slipped the rope from the ring in her halter, impatiently hurrying her through smoke toward the door. He could hear voices now and the thump of boots, and stopped with a curse, hand bound for his sixshooter. But the hand instead smashed into a nosebag and suddenly he saw how with luck he might fool them.

All the fire he saw was at the barn's far side. It would still be dark outside this door.

Keeping hold of her halter, he caught up the feed bag, pulling her head around till he could reach her tail. She whinnied more urgent and the trust in that wrung a fresh groan from Jade—but he had to do this if he was to get clear.

Snatching a fistful of tail hair, he twisted it round the strap of the bag, fetching the canvas up close to her rump; she didn't mind now but would when it thumped her. In foal and excited by the fire as well, when that bag flapped behind her, she'd take off like a rocket.

The hunters' racket was not far off when he pointed the mare toward the opening and yelled. The flat of his hand hit her hard on the rump and she went through the door like hell wouldn't hold her.

A shout went up. A gun hammered its staccato sound into the night. A second man added his fire to the uproar while the mare's flogging hoofs rushed the timbered slope.

All over the yard, Jade could hear men yelling. "Fiersen!" one cried, not ten yards from the door. "Bastard got clean away—get the horses, Chelly!" And someone else shouted, "Wasn't Joe claimin' there was *two* horses in there? Where's the other'n?"

Holding his breath, Fiersen grimly waited.

"Hell with it," snarled Rubelcaba's crew boss. "C'mon—we gotta make sure he keeps goin'!"

For another ten heart pounds, Fiersen stayed where he was, but the stallion's frenzied attempts to get free set him dousing a feed sack in the mare's tub of water and turned him toward the stud's blazing stall. The big black looked half out of his head. One leg had a gash from a splintered board and smoke showed in patches on his hide where sparks had dropped from the burning loft. What with the shouting and horse sounds outside, and the wind-rushed roar of flames all around him, the animal paid scant attention to Fiersen. Deep in panic, he kept swinging his head, lunging and kicking, as he tried to break loose.

The Spanish Cross crew tore out of the yard, larruping after the runaway mare.

Jade studied the horse. Soothing talk failed to reach through its terror. He was in the last stall on this side; his frantic kicking had half demolished it. Fiersen kept talking; the animal stopped kicking. Turning his head far as the rope would let him, he looked at Fiersen with the whites of his eyes. Without recognition.

The horse began pawing the floor. Fiersen

kept talking. "Whoa, now—whoa, boy!" kept edging nearer, hoping if he could get a hand on him to quiet him; but a couple near misses from steel shod hoofs sent him backing away again. No chance that way.

He would have to get in through the stall's broken side, a pretty uninviting notion. Jade moved into the next stall, picking his way through splintered boards, still talking, getting closer. A couple of planks still hung from a joist that went into the rafters from between the feed boxes and, with some effort, he wrenched these loose. He slipped the drying sack from his shoulder, trampled it into a puddle on the floor, all that was left of the stallion's water. Up with it suddenly he made a swift pass that shut off the animal's sight and brought the loose ends through the halter and hoped to hell it would stay where he'd put it.

He had to work fast. The leap of those flames was terribly close, and the lung scalding heat. The loft overhead was a blazing inferno and, even with his head wetly swathed in the sack, the big black was trembling.

Precious moments were lost while Fiersen picked at the knots which kept the horse anchored to the wall ring. They were like dried parfleche, so tight had the animal jerked them. Fiersen's hands seemed all thumbs in this terrible pressure. At last they came free; then, just as he was ready to back the horse out, a loft board came down in a red shower of sparks and the stud lunged against him, squealing with fear.

Groaning, Fiersen kept his feet. Singed flesh, burnt hair made an acrid stench but somehow he managed to get the horse clear. With an arm thrown up before his eyes, Fiersen stumbled out into the belly of the barn. Back and forth he staggered with the led horse sidling while more planks fell and the roar of the flames was all about them. Wind snatched back the smoke and through streaming eyes, Jade glimpsed the door hole and, gasping, half cooked, he dragged the horse through.

TWENTY-SEVEN

THERE WAS JUST one thing left to do as Jade saw it. All the mental trails he'd explored came smack up against the same hard wall. Nothing would stop Rubelcaba but death. And so he had come here to kill the man.

Lamps in the Spanish Cross headquarters

drove yellow bars across the black gallery as Fiersen drew rein and sent his hail banging off the walls.

The cook stuck his head from the mess shack door. "Nobody home—only me!"

"Where's Rubelcaba?"

"Town, I reckon. Somebody sent fer him an'—"

Fiersen was already gone, leaving nothing behind but the settling dust, the *rataplan-rataplan-rat* of his travel as the black stallion carried him away toward Dry Bottom.

Slank Calder, in the Hairpin House lobby, with a catlike grin got up out of his chair when he saw Rubelcaba step through the door.

"Clear out," Rubelcaba growled at the clerk, and fetched his suspicious look back to Calder. "What are *you* doin' here?"

"Linin' myself up with the law and order crowd—I've quit Bar D. Figured you might like to know. You can spread the word I've took all I kin stomach; they're a bunch of damn rustlers," Calder said with a laugh. "I'm here to give you the lowdown on Fiersen. About how he's workin' these steals an' all—how he vents the brands on them run off cattle, rebrands an' sells 'em as Bar

D stuff right out in the open to the stock-yards at Tucson. Even had me in charge of sellin' 'em, by God—but I'm onto him now!"

Calder winked. "You kin check on the dates an' numbers with Tarlton . . . An' one other thing. I found Vance buried back of Bar D's barn. Case of lead poisonin'. You don't look a heap surprised," he chuckled.

Rubelcaba said, with no sign of pleasure, "Ain't you kind of rushin' things, Calder?"

"When I seen your crew squattin' out in the trees I didn't reckon so." He said with a soft half smiling negligence: "You wasn't figurin' to trap me too, was you?"

Rubelcaba, restless, looked balked and mean. But his loud bass laugh sounded jovial enough. "I don't forget my friends, Slank. I make it a point to take care of obligations. You've risked your neck to get at the truth of this and I'll make sure the sheriff gets the right slant. Where you stayin'?"

"Right here," Calder nodded with plenty of meaning.

The Spanish Cross owner took another hard look at him. "I'm meetin' a feller here on business directly—"

"Anything you got to say to Jim Tarlton can be said in front of me. It was me suggested he send fer you. I've told him my notions about them cattle an' he figures I've got the straight of it; said he's been suspectin' somethin' like that—even thought I mighta been in on it, which is somethin' you got to git ironed out pronto. I been duped by Jade Fiersen till you'd hardly believe it—you kin set folks straight. Best I kin think of to show you're back of me all the way."

His face held a sly and knowing grin. "You need my help cleanin' up this valley. I kin help you figure which is the goats. Now you take that guy Tabbs. He looks like a rustler—an' Teke, don't you reckon? That feller fair gives me the creepin' willies. My notion Teke an' Fiersen is in this together."

He went back and sat down with a comfortable sigh. "What you need is a gent you kin depend on."

Rubelcaba smiled. "Meanin' you I suppose."

"Meanin' me," Calder said. "Just before I left Bar D this evenin', I picked up a little item may interest you. About Fiersen. I'll let you know when I've got to the bottom of it—has to do with a letter . . ."

"What he's been up to right here in this valley will hang him plenty high enough fer me. I understand he's taken to the hills, but we'll roust him out."

"You won't need to bother," a quiet voice said. "You can start your roustin' any time you're ready."

Michael Strawn was through with Bar D. Free at last of restraint and loyalty; free of everything but his thoughts. It was his thoughts made him scowl. He could quit this damn country—ride straight out of it. But he was finding he couldn't ride away from himself.

Traveling these timbered uplands it had begun to come over him that quitting Jade Fiersen hadn't much altered anything. He was still bitterly faced with the same ugly issues, same personalities, the same burning angers and hateful suspicions which had driven him away from Jade's headquarters. He was no better satisfied now than he had been.

Twisting round in the saddle, he sent a dour look back over the miles, trying to pick up a last view of the ranch that had been all the home he had ever known. It was cut off from him now like everything else he had put between. Much as he despised Fiersen, he was glad he'd come away before his temper had turned him to gunplay; he was glad because once Jade had been his best friend.

It wasn't altogether Cherry Grant's fault Mike had ceased to respect Jade Fiersen; she was only responsible for his hate. They had all grown up together, all three of them, and for long as he could remember Strawn had been in love with Cherry.

Not that he'd ever said much about it; he had observed it was Jade the girl cared for. He'd long been resigned to that part. What he couldn't get over was the way Fiersen treated her. The man owed her *some*thing certainly; he should have done the right thing and married her. The fact that he hadn't was why Strawn hated him. And despised him because the man was willing, lying down, to take anything Rubelcaba handed him.

"Must have good reason to keep his trap shut," was the way Mike had to look at it. "And whatever the reason it can't be no square one—there ain't nothin' square about him no more."

Getting late, he noticed. Not that he was hungry; didn't reckon he ever would be hungry again. Might just as well keep pushing right along; maybe time he got out of this country he could set about forgetting. New scenes, new faces—that was the ticket. New problems to crowd out the old.

It was getting near to twilight. Cherry, he recalled, had always liked this hour. The sun was gone off the valley now. A hush hung over the sparse timber and juniper. It was a time when a man shoved back from the table to roll up a smoke.

A sound brought Strawn abruptly out of his thinking. He stopped the horse with a hand on its nostrils. Trees seemed thicker off yonder. Eyeing the drift of shadows over there, Strawn's stare narrowed. When faint horse sound filtered down from that direction, he reached for his rifle, ears cocked, listening.

Horses meant men and there seemed damn little reason why men should be here. This was Bar D range, jumbled foothills seldom used and never patrolled in Strawn's memory. He was downwind from those sounds he had caught, so he dropped from the saddle, tied his mount to a scraggly scrub cedar and quietly worked his way through the brush.

The ground tilted down when he came through the trees. He reached a point where he found himself peering into what looked to be a small hidden valley. About two miles across, he judged and, not far off, close to the near edge of it, he spied a shack with two-three men hunkered side of it. Three in sight and three tied horses, and one of this batch Strawn recognized. Teke, Vance's Turkey Track foreman. Off on the level land, entirely untended, was a dark blotch of cattle.

Only one answer to this in Mike's mind. To a man brought up as Strawn had been, the whole look of this place spelled *rustlers*. And when a man found rustlers working his range, he didn't waste time asking questions. He did what Strawn was proposing to do when he got down flat in the grass on his belly and lined up the shack in the sights of his rifle.

It was a good heavy gun and he knew how to use it. His first shot tagged the man by the door. His second took Teke like paper in the wind and knocked him sprawling heels over head. His third caught the last man running.

He blew the smoke from his rifle and stayed where he was awaiting further developments. Satisfied there weren't going to be any, he got his horse and rode on down there.

Man by the door needed no attention, nor did the one who had tried to light a shuck out of there. Teke was still in the quick, though how long he would be seemed a matter of minutes.

Strawn fetched him a drink and squatted with his back up against the shack's wall to get what comfort he could while waiting. "No use dirtying a shirt tail with you. When that sun drops behind the rimrocks, you'll be just as dead as them other two snakes."

He bit off a chunk of eating tobacco, considering the dying Teke without favor. "You got anything to say, you'd best be at it."

Teke had.

When Strawn climbed aboard his horse, there was considerable change in his whole appearance.

Fiersen said, "Best get on with it," coming a little away from the door, moving to one side to put solid wall behind him. Calder, settled deep in his chair, hardly seemed to breathe.

Malevolence thinned Rubelcaba's cheeks. "By God, you've got your guts, comin' here!"

"Didn't expect you to like it. You ain't

going to like any part of this, Burr." Jade considered the man, dark and quiet. "Get a pen and some paper—"

"That won't change nothin'," Rubelcaba sneered. "Who the hell you think would believe it? You ain't pullin' no weight around here. Not no more, you ain't—not even had Calder never opened his mouth. An' he sure as hell has. He's been tellin' me—"

"We'll be coming to Slank later. Right now," Fiersen said, "I'm dealin' with you. You goin' to write what I tell you?"

"No, by God!" Rubelcaba snarled.

"Guess we can wait for Tarlton if you want. Won't help you much, but we can wait, I reckon." Fiersen hooked both thumbs in the belt at his waist. "Before you quit this room, Rubelcaba, you're going to write out a full confession—"

"Haw, haw, haw!" Rubelcaba laughed. "You're a real card, you are!"

"Or," Fiersen said, "you can go for your gun."

"Why, you two-bit owlhooter," Rubelcaba cried. "You cut your string too short this time! Half the boys in your outfit'll turn state's evidence an' help yank the rope when it's round your neck!"

"I wouldn't be surprised," Fiersen told

him dryly. "But that won't help *you*. I'm not expectin' to get out of here alive and I don't expect you to walk out of here, either."

Rubelcaba stiffened, took a backward step with his eyes bright slits. He was that way, tensed to reach for his pistol, when Tarlton's voice whipped across from the diningroom door. "Hold it right there! One move, Fiersen, and you'll be too dead to skin!"

He stepped into the room with Cantlicker, the storekeeper, Tabbs and several others crowding back of him. The barrel of his gun pointed squarely at Fiersen.

Jade's face didn't change but Rubelcaba's did. He said, "Nice work, boys," with a vast satisfaction. His chin jumped forward as he stared at Fiersen. "Now we'll see whose hide gits nailed." And Calder sprang out of his chair like a cat.

"Rangers is huntin' him under the name of Will Carver for killin' a marshal—"

"That's purely a lie!" Taisy cried from the top of the stairs, and came flying down, flushed and excitedly waving a paper. "It says right here in this letter Frank had that that marshal was shot in the back by Sam Ketchum!"

A startled silence came over the room. Cantlicker broke it, hurrying over to the girl. "We ain't tryin' him fer that—" Rubelcaba began, but Cantlicker frowningly waved him quiet. "She's right," he said, after having peered at it. "This here's a sworn statement, notarized and witnessed—"

"Hell with that!" Calder started forward. "We've got enough on him fer what he's done here to hang the bastard forty times over!" and raised his voice: "What the hell we waitin' fer?"

"That's right," someone growled, "he's the bugger we want." And Tarlton, the brand man, watchfully careful, reached around Fiersen and stepped clear with his pistol. The man didn't even seem to have noticed. He was staring as though stunned at Endite's letter in Cantlicker's hand.

Fiercely eyeing Rubelcaba, Taisy cried, "You can't do this! You know might well Jade's not a rustler! You—"

With an oath, Rubelcaba flung her out of his way, but Taisy flew across the room. She flung an arm around Fiersen, clinging defiantly; and when she spun away there was a gun in his hand. Frank's little belly gun, its muzzle unwaveringly turned on Rubelcaba, the rancher's face gone the color of wood ash.

Fiersen said, "It's just got one slug but that slug's got your name on it, Burr—start shootin'!"

It was Tarlton who fired. Taisy screamed when she saw Jade stagger. Rubelcaba's hand flashed like lightning just as Strawn's head and shoulders came through the room's west window. Strawn's first shot knocked Jim Tarlton sprawling. Rubelcaba's gun tipped up and flame lanced out of its muzzle whitely; and Taisy saw Fiersen shudder. His knees folded under him and pitched him forward and one outthrust hand took his weight, holding it in suspension. Slowly, terribly, he began to crawl, mocking eyes on Rubelcaba.

The rancher fired again but Fiersen kept crawling and a cold gray horror looked from Rubelcaba's stare. That was when Fiersen lifted Frank's derringer and shot him. Amazement twisted the ranchman's face and he clutched at his chest, half turned and died.

Two days later when Fiersen opened his eyes, he found himself peering into Taisy's wide stare. Doc told him bluntly, "You've had a good nurse." It was obvious, however, neither one of them heard him, being too absorbed, he guessed, with what each one of them read in the other's look.

The old doc chuckled. "Reckon he'll pull out of it with her fussin' over him. This valley will be proud to neighbor with him," he said to himself, "after the way Slank Calder's been singing to high heaven. Funny thing about that—never put a hand near his pistol that night. Plumb yellow, I expect. Feller'd have to be, I reckon, to treat the mother of his child the way he's treated Cherry. She'll be all right, now that Mike Strawn's figuring to tie the knot with her. Taisy sure bowled them over when she got a good look at that brand inspector's hands and jumped all over him for killing Frank Endite. Better for him if Mike's shot had finished him."

He picked up his bag and headed for the bar.

Fiersen held up Taisy's hand. "Only one thing wrong with this batch of fingers. Quick's I can get up out of this bed, we'll take the night stage to Tucson and get that tended to. They've got a preacher up there you'll purely like."

The publishers hope that this
Large Print Book has brought
you pleasurable reading.
Each title is designed to make
the text as easy to see as possible.
G.K. Hall Large Print Books
are available from your library and
your local bookstore. Or, you can
receive information by mail on
upcoming and current Large Print Books
and order directly from the publishers.
Just send your name and address to:

G.K. Hall & Co.
70 Lincoln Street
Boston, Mass. 02111

or call, toll-free:

1-800-343-2806

A note on the text
Large print edition designed by
Pauline L. Chin.
Composed in 16 pt. Plantin
on a Xyvision 300/Linotron 202N
by Tara Casey
of G.K. Hall & Co.